PENGUIN BOOKS

A CAGE OF DESIRES

Shuchi Singh Kalra is the Amazon bestselling author of two novels—*Done with Men* and *I'm Big. So What!?* Her short stories have appeared in *Love across Borders*, *Stories for Your Valentine* and *NAW Anthology 2013*. In her freelancing career of over a decade, Shuchi has written for major print and online publications such as *Femina*, *Good Housekeeping*, *Hotelier International*, *Huffington Post* and *Home Review*, among others. She has also been listed among the top women authors to follow on Twitter.

Website: www.shuchikalra.com
Facebook: facebook.com/shuchisinghkalra/
Twitter: @shuchikalra

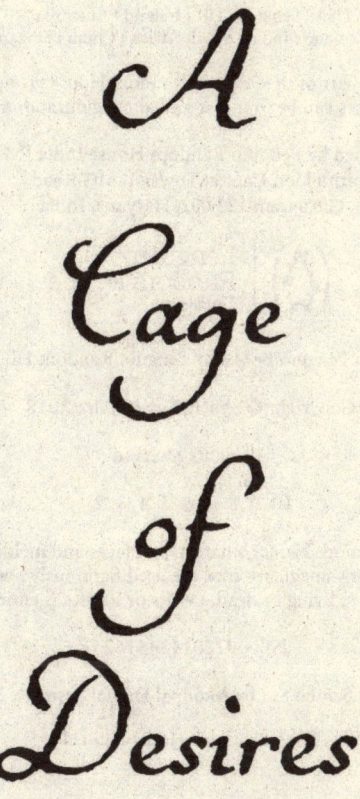

A Cage of Desires

SHUCHI SINGH KALRA

PENGUIN BOOKS

An imprint of Penguin Random House

PENGUIN BOOKS

USA | Canada | UK | Ireland | Australia
New Zealand | India | South Africa | China | Singapore

Penguin Books is part of the Penguin Random House group of companies
whose addresses can be found at global.penguinrandomhouse.com

Published by Penguin Random House India Pvt. Ltd
4th Floor, Capital Tower 1, MG Road,
Gurugram 122 002, Haryana, India

First published in Penguin Books by Penguin Random House India 2018

10 9 8 7 6 5 4 3 2

ISBN 9780143441625

Typeset in Bembo Std by Manipal Digital Systems, Manipal

Printed at Repro India Limited

www.penguin.co.in

MIX
Paper from
responsible sources
FSC® C047271

To every phoenix who rose from the ashes . . .

You are my every dream
You are my every nightmare

You are the fire in my night sky
You are the darkness in my sparkle

You are my oasis of peace
Yet all my demons look like you

PROLOGUE

'Aneisha!' Renu called out from the doorstep. 'Dinner is ready.'

Renu always looked forward to these rare instances when her children managed to take a break from their busy schedules and visit her at her little cottage in the hills. Avi got bored here quickly, because he could not find much to do but Aneisha loved staying over for as long as she could. The mother and daughter would sit outside in the lawn under the gentle winter sun and chat for hours. She shared everything with her mother. Mihir would drop by often, and even though Aneisha knew of her mother's relationship with him, she never questioned it. 'Tell me whenever you are comfortable, Maa,' she had said chirpily that one time when Renu tried to explain Mihir's presence in her life. Avi had not been too pleased with Mihir's closeness with his mother initially but as he came to know him better, his apprehensions gradually faded away and they had grown to be friendlier now. Aneisha, of course, had a role to play in reshaping his perspective and it made Renu smile every time she remembered how her daughter had done it so cleverly. The younger of the two siblings, Avi had always been more possessive of his mother, but Aneisha had—over many months and many conversations—made him aware of his mother's emotional needs. He had gradually come to understand that Renu was more than his mother—she was a woman in her own right, and she needed love and companionship too.

'Aneisha!' Renu called out again when she did not get a reply. She walked out into the lawn and saw her sitting on the garden swing with her phone pressed against her ears and tears streaming down her cheeks.

Renu knew it wasn't her turn to speak. At least not yet. She waited patiently for Aneisha to finish her call before walking up to her and taking a place beside her on the swing. Without asking or saying anything, she gathered her daughter into a tight embrace. Aneisha buried her face into her mother's chest and cried softly.

'Do you want to talk about it?' Renu asked once Aneisha's sobs had subsided.

'There's this guy, Maa,' Aneisha started and Renu listened intently. Her daughter was twenty-five and so far, she had never been in a serious relationship, at least not one that Renu was aware of. This must be a special one, she thought.

'Did you have a fight with him?' Renu was curious and anxious about the boy in her daughter's life but she wanted to approach the topic cautiously, without being too intrusive.

'It's not just one fight, Maa. He hurts me. He deliberately hurts me—mentally, emotionally, in every possible way!' Aneisha sobbed.

'Then why is he still in your life?' Renu asked, now very worried. Her little girl seemed deeply wounded, scarred and heartbroken.

'Because I love him, Maa,' Aneisha whispered, almost apologetically. Renu felt a dull ache in her heart as harrowing memories of Arjun came flooding back to her mind. Those memories were long dead and buried, the scars had dried up and faded but there were times they still ached and tugged at her soul like a festering wound. Renu had accepted it as the price she had to pay for her hard-earned wisdom but her daughter's helpless tears mortified her. She had been to hell and back, but come what may, she had resolved to never let her daughter walk down the path of terrifying darkness that she herself had treaded.

'Let's go inside, Aneisha. We'll sit there and talk, okay? I have something to tell you,' Renu said and helped Aneisha up, holding her tenderly by the shoulder. What she was going to do was perhaps one of the most difficult things she'd ever done but she could not keep quiet now. Her daughter's life and happiness were at stake.

She sat Aneisha down once they were inside the house and then she told her everything about the men in her life—the kind of relationships she had with them and what those relationships taught her. Words poured out from the deep graves in her soul. She did not hold back any details. Aneisha listened intently without saying much but her face changed even as her mother spoke. She could only imagine the heartbreaking agony of the trials and tribulations her mother had gone through.

'Did it make any sense at all?' Renu asked softly when she was done narrating everything she had to.

'Yes, Maa, it does. A lot of sense. And it makes me see the future of my relationship,' Aneisha said firmly, trying hard not to choke, her beautiful eyes wide.

Renu smiled at her. 'Show. Don't tell—that's what the best storytellers do, don't they?' No matter how close she was to her daughter, she really wasn't expecting Aneisha to part ways with a man she loved solely on her mother's advice. 'You are wise beyond your years, Aneisha. You always have been. Never accept less than what you deserve,' she said. *Never accept less than what you deserve.* Renu had spent a lifetime learning that lesson on her own, but her daughter understood the depth of that statement immediately. After dinner, she stepped outside to make a call and in five minutes she walked in with a wide smile on her face.

A tear trickled down Renu's cheek as she hugged her daughter tightly.

ONE

'Renu! Renu! Where are you?' Kishan Kumar's coarse voice boomed across the living room.

'Yes, Bauji!' Renu scampered out of the kitchen, her hands coated in flour and forehead punctuated with beads of sweat. Even after almost two decades of living under the same roof, she was not comfortable with this authoritarian cranky old man, her father-in-law. 'What happened, Bauji?' she asked nervously, because whenever he called out to her like that, it rarely spelt good news.

'Why don't you ask your daughter?' he said, glaring at Aneisha who stood cowering by the table, her head hung low.

'Aneisha?' Renu looked at her sixteen-year-old daughter who was on the verge of tears. Her silky black hair fell loosely around her beautiful oval face, which now seemed pale with distress.

'Aneisha, what did you do?' she repeated, louder this time. For whatever she did, Aneisha would be better off being reprimanded by her. At least that would save her from Bauji's caustic tongue, which could inflict wounds that took years to heal.

'This . . . this is what she has been up to . . . instead of studying for her board exams!' roared Bauji as he flung a book on the floor. It landed face-up and the cover read, *Kiss of a Stranger* by Maya. Renu's face flushed and she wiped it with the edge of her cotton sari.

'I am sorry, Maa, a friend gave it to me,' explained Aneisha, her voice loaded with guilt as if she'd committed a sin.

'Just go to your room,' Renu ordered Aneisha in a stern voice. The girl quickly made her way out.

'It is only natural for a young girl to be curious about sex and sensuality. What is the big deal?' she was tempted to retaliate, but she knew all too well how her father-in-law felt about such things.

'I'm very sorry about this, Bauji. I'll talk to her . . .' she said instead, her voice trembling.

'Yes. You'd better! Girls from good families don't read filthy books like these. What kind of values have you been giving her?' he said in his usual accusatory tone. This wasn't the first time he had made an indirect and hurtful reference to her 'values', which in his opinion were scarce because she came from a broken home.

Throughout her life, Renu had shouldered the burden of something that wasn't her fault at all—her parents' divorce, a turbulent childhood, a lost youth and now, accusations that put her under scrutiny all the time. For Bauji, her background was a taboo. Dev sympathized and had been compassionate in that regard at least, although that didn't stop him from being patronizing and condescending towards her often because he thought she understood little about the workings of a 'healthy Indian family'.

Renu would stay silent whenever this happened. Through the years she had learnt the hard way that silence was her best defence. Only when Bauji had stormed back to his room and banged the door shut angrily behind him, did she dare to pick up the book from its place on the ground. She caressed the cover softly with her palm.

Maya. That name had been making waves for quite some time now.

~

'Where did you get this book from?' Renu casually asked Aneisha in the privacy of her room.

'I'm really sorry, Maa . . .' Aneisha wailed, ready to cry if reprimanded.

'You don't have to be sorry, *beta*, it is a natural part of growing up. When I was your age, I used to love reading romantic novels,' she said with a smile.

'Really?' Aneisha's eyes lit up with curiosity. She could never imagine her staid mother losing herself in steamy stories.

'Yes, my baby,' Renu placed a comforting hand on Aneisha's shoulder. 'My friends and I, we used to borrow those Mills & Boons books from a local library and read them in school, during recess, sometimes even during classes. And you know how strict convent schools are? Once, Sister Martha caught us and made us run ten rounds of the football field on a hot summer afternoon! She probably thought she could get it all out of our system,' she chuckled and Aneisha joined in. She still found it hard to believe that her docile mother had a rebellious streak hidden within her, but the confession comforted her and made her feel a little less guilty. 'I know you love to read and you should . . . as many kinds of books as you can . . . each book has something to teach you,' she continued.

'Then why did Daadu . . . ?' Aneisha's face grew sullen as she remembered what had happened a few moments ago.

'Beta, everyone has their own opinion, their own ideology. Daadu is from a different generation and a little conservative and we can do nothing to change him at this age. But you do whatever makes you happy. Just make sure he doesn't find out,' she winked at her daughter. Raising a teen is not an easy job, she sighed.

'Thank you, Maa!' Aneisha gave her mother a heartfelt hug.

'But don't waste too much time on these right now. You can read all you want after your board exams, okay?' Renu said and stroked her daughter's lustrous hair fondly. Aneisha looked so much like her. Her enormous almond-shaped eyes twinkled when she laughed and her raven-black locks had a will of their own; nothing could hold them back. Every time she tried to tie them up, they would rebelliously spring back and tease her cheeks in defiance. The mother–daughter duo shared plenty of intrinsic qualities too. Just like her mother, Aneisha was sensitive, intuitive and wise beyond her years. She was by and large an obedient child, but the spark of occasional rebelliousness in her eyes was hard to miss.

Renu reminisced about the days when she was Aneisha's age, when she would drown herself in sensual romances, to experience a world of lure that was so compelling, and so forbidden. Back then, it was a flight of fantasy, but now it was an urgent escape from the dreary realities of her life. However, no matter how supportive she wanted to be of her daughter, her understanding did not come without its fair share of apprehension. Aneisha was at a tender age—a crossroads—where whatever she learnt and absorbed from the world around her now, would shape her as the woman she was going to be for the rest of her life. Renu did not want to hold her back the way she had been restrained. She wanted to hold Aneisha's hand while she explored the myriad mysteries the world had to offer. From where she stood, it seemed difficult but Renu was determined to be the wind beneath her daughter's wings.

'Mama . . . look what I made!' Avinash, her ten-year-old son, came cruising into the room with a wooden object that bore at least a faint resemblance, if not much, to an aeroplane.

'That's very nice. Does it fly?' she asked, her gaze fondly following the energetic little boy who scampered all around the place.

'Not on its own, Mama, but I can make it fly like this!' He ran around her in circles tirelessly, with his creation held as high as his little dirt-covered hands would allow. The boy was obsessed with aeroplanes. There was a remote-control operated one that he had been pestering her for and she badly wanted to gift it to him on his birthday next month, but Dev hadn't sanctioned the money for it yet.

She couldn't quite remember the last time she had an honest, real conversation with her husband—he was hardly ever there, especially since he'd taken up that job in Sitapur. It always bothered Renu. People migrated from Sitapur to Lucknow in search of jobs. She had not known anyone who had done it the other way round.

'Why don't you look for something here? It doesn't matter if the salary is a little lesser,' she had once hesitatingly suggested, but he did not feel the need to explain even once why he wasn't trying hard enough to stay closer to his wife, children and his ageing father. He wasn't a bad husband or an irresponsible father, it was just that he did not share enough with her. Actually, he did not share anything with her . . . his thoughts, his emotions, his decisions, his body. She wasn't privy to any of those.

'You just take good care of Bauji, the kids and the house. Don't bother about the rest. I'll take care of it,' he politely told her on more than one occasion. And for so many years, that's all she had been doing . . . until last year.

The last time Dev had come home, she'd told him that she wanted to buy that remote-controlled aeroplane for

Avi but he had just nodded and mumbled some incoherent words without giving any definitive reply. It had been weeks now, and she had almost decided to tap into her secret piggy bank—the one she had been feeding all these years.

A temporary silence enveloped the room as Aneisha went back to her studies and Avi scampered into the yard with his precious toy plane. She cast a furtive glance at the mirror and a pair of lacklustre eyes and a worn-down middle-aged face devoid of any emotions stared back at her. The brutal reminder that she looked older than most women her age stabbed at her heart and made her want to move away from the mirror. She tucked a loose lock behind her ear and shook her head disappointedly. Closing the door, she absent-mindedly picked up the bright red paperback lying on her bed that she had recently confiscated from her daughter. The cover depicted a silhouette of two young bodies entwined intimately. How tastefully done, she thought as she flicked the pages.

'*She moaned and arched her back as he penetrated her being, but her voice was muffled under a forceful, almost violent kiss. His tongue hungrily explored the insides of her demanding mouth as she thrust her pelvis towards him, slapping his buttocks as she did, urging him to go faster, harder . . . to be rough,*' read a random passage. Renu smiled to herself and hid the book on her bookshelf that was already bursting with books—big and small, old and new. They were her most prized possessions, her only companions during long, lonely nights. They were her secret escape route, her utopia.

As she lay in bed, she felt a familiar ache between her legs, which made an appearance ever too often. Sometimes her imagination and her fingers would calm her down eventually but at other times, it would persist, refusing to go away, like today. She got up and stumbled to her cupboard to gather her tools of catharsis.

TWO

'Tsk. Tsk. What has this world come to?' grumbled Bauji as he read an excerpt from Maya's book that was featured in the Sunday edition of his favourite newspaper.

'If he hates it so much, why is he reading it at all?' Renu muttered angrily to herself as she went about clearing the lower part of the table where old newspapers had been piling up for an entire week. She smirked inwardly as Bauji carried on with his customary rants, wondering how he would react if he found out about her collection of Maya's books stashed in the cupboard. Those books were her little secret—her indulgence, her transitory escape from the dreary reality. Maya's words gave wings to her own deepest, most intimate thoughts, especially when the evenings got too lonely. One couldn't blame her father-in-law either—Maya was an enigma that sparked extreme feelings in anyone who read her. You could either love

her or hate her, but you could never be indifferent to
her. While some loved Maya for the bold, steamy style
of her writing, others hated her for being so brazen and
unapologetic about sex and sensuality. She wasn't catering
to a niche either—the three novels she had released so far
had been national bestsellers, lapped up eagerly by readers
and non-readers alike. You couldn't label them porn but
they were nothing short of it in any way. The critics had
called her the 'Queen of Erotica', and incidentally, that was
what the special Sunday feature was about: Women who
are reinventing the concept of sensuality in India.

Along with Maya, it featured a couple of women
directors and an artist. Their strong, confident faces smiled
back from the glossy pages of the newspaper, except
for Maya's. Nobody knew her and she never gave any
interviews, but of all these women, she was the one who
made the most news and ruffled the most feathers.

Renu kept to her business, deciding not to respond to
her father-in-law's barbs but he was far from done. 'These
women are corrupting our Indian culture. Shameless!
How do they face their families after all this?' he went on,
talking to no one in particular. Everybody knew *Maya* was
a fictitious name but nobody knew the real woman behind
those racy, raunchy romances. There had been many
rumours that Maya was actually a man; but then how did
he know so much about that part of a woman's mind where
uninhibited sexual fantasies take wing? How could he dive
into the deep carrels and crypts of a woman's heart where
she hid all her dark intimate secrets? Most women would

shy away from acknowledging them, leave alone allowing their thoughts to flow onto paper in such candid words. All the speculation and curiosity only added to the enigma of Maya.

~

The old desktop in her room spluttered painfully as Renu struggled to type out an email. She gave the CPU a good, hard thump on the side but that didn't help much. The poor machine wheezed from the strain—it was way past its prime. In a feeble attempt to revive it from its paralysis, she decided to clear the browser history, but what she saw made her eyes widen with surprise. The browser history had various permutations and combinations of: Maya, erotica, romance novel, India, official website.

Who could it be? she thought, perplexed. Who in this family was so fascinated with Maya? Aneisha had her own laptop and Avi was too young for this. And Bauji, well he didn't even know how to switch on a computer. It could be none other than Dev. But why was Dev so intrigued and obsessed with Maya? But then again, wasn't every other man who had read her books? It would be rather out of character for someone as staid as Dev though, she thought, to actually read erotica. She'd never seen him reading anything apart from newspapers and magazines, which is why his curiosity about Maya seemed even more baffling to Renu. She sighed and hit the delete button.

Unlike most authors who revelled in the public eye, Maya did not have any website or even a blog. Her books were everywhere—on the publisher's website, Amazon and Flipkart, but no one knew who Maya actually was. Review portals were flooded with mixed reactions to her books. Some were glowing reviews, whereas some berated her books, but there was never any promotional attempt from her side. She was nowhere to be found, an enigma that did not seem to even exist.

Thinking of Dev took her back to the last time he had come home. He had spent the day with the children, helping Aneisha with maths and listening patiently to Avi as he rambled on about his hand-made flying wonder.

At the Kumar household, Sunday was usually a cleaning day, unlike other households where families went out for a movie or to a restaurant, or just relaxed at home with a Sunday special meal. But this time, he had surprised her by taking them for an outing to the famous Hazratganj market. The children were thrilled. 'It will be a welcome break for the children,' he had said.

Renu had draped a mustard yellow georgette saree that was an anniversary gift from Dev years ago. He had said that the colour looked beautiful on her. She recollected how happy it had made her feel back then. The thin, wispy fabric clung to her curves, which, on most days, stayed hidden under loose-fitting cotton salwar-kameez or cotton sarees that didn't come in the way of her house work. She put a sparkling yellow and silver bindi on her forehead and lined her lips with a crimson red lipstick, secretly hoping Dev would notice but he quickly ushered them all into the car without so much as an appreciative glance. The market was closed since it was a Sunday but they enjoyed a round of *gol-gappa*s, and gorged on *aloo tikki*, *papdi chaat* and *kulfi*. Renu looked on as Avi and Aneisha shared an ice cream and a rare sense of peace and contentment had filled her heart. Since Bauji had stayed home, she had finally been able to relax.

'Is Aneisha paying attention to her other subjects as well?' Dev asked as they sat on a wrought iron bench facing the fountain in the middle of Hazratganj. 'I want her to score at least 95 per cent.'

'She's working hard. Don't worry, she'll do well,' Renu replied with a smile.

He nodded.

'Avi is growing naughtier by the day,' she continued, trying hard to keep the awkward silence from creeping in. A young couple on the bench opposite theirs laughed out loud and the woman sank her face into the man's chest. Renu looked longingly at her husband, who was now signalling the children to come back. It was late in the evening and it was time to go home. 'Let's go. Bauji must be waiting for dinner.'

That night she had slid a reluctant hand between the buttons of his shirt but he turned to the other side and closed his eyes, mumbling that he was too tired.

Renu found that odd. Did he not desire her at all? Did he desire Maya? She knew that she was not fantasy material but she was his wife, and the mother of his children. She knew she could please him too . . . if only he'd let her.

THREE

'Have we run out of salt in this house?' Bauji asked sarcastically as he pushed a morsel past his dentures. Aneisha quickly passed him the sprinkler before he had a chance to say anything else. She looked past him at her mother. Renu mouthed a silent *thank you* and smiled at her daughter. She was glad to have someone cover up for her but why had she forgotten to season the vegetables? It wasn't like her to be absent-minded around the house. Try as she might, her thoughts kept drifting back to the browser history. Why was her husband so in awe of Maya? She never knew he read her books—at least he hadn't told her, just like so many other things. Was he actually searching for her? And what would he do if he found her? It was a disturbing thought and she feared that the seemingly unlikely event would turn her life upside down.

At the Kumar household, dinner was usually served by 8 p.m. after which Bauji would retire before the TV and the children would be tucked in bed. But by the time Renu got done with clearing the table and preparing for the next day, it would be past 11 p.m. Her muscles ached and her head throbbed. That night, she drew out a few sheets of paper and started scribbling, like she did almost every night. It was the only way for her to vent her frustrations. The regret of giving up a career, the burden of a loveless marriage, the thankless drudgery she went through each day, the unfulfilled desires. With deft strokes of her pen, she transformed the ugly realities of her life into beautiful prose. Many a time, she had toyed with the idea of maintaining an online journal but somehow, it wasn't half as intimate as the relationship she shared with a pen and paper. For her, it was a simplistic solution to the most complex of her problems.

A knock on the door interrupted her flow. She quickly bunched up the loose sheets of paper and stuffed them under the pillow, before she opened the door. 'Mama, I want to sleep with you,' said Avi, his eyes groggy with sleep.

'Okay, beta,' she readily agreed. The boy snuggled beside his mother and comforted by her familiar scent, slowly drifted into peaceful slumber. Renu covered him with a quilt and pulled out the paper she had shoved carelessly under the pillow. She was relieved it wasn't Bauji. She ironed out the crinkles on the sheet of papers with the warmth of her palm and immersed herself back in the words she had abandoned midway. It took ten sheets and two hours, but once she had flushed every ounce of emotion from within her on to those sheets of paper, she was able to go to bed with a lighter heart.

~

It was almost noon when Renu returned home. She had been out since morning. 'Where are you coming from at this hour?' Bauji growled, his eyes brimming with irritation.

'Bauji, I had to go to the market to get some things for the children. Some books and stationery . . .' she said, wondering why she had to justify everything she ever did, especially to him. She was thirty-seven and had spent the last eighteen years of her life as Dev's wife, yet she had not earned the freedom to do anything in this house on her own terms.

Sometimes she wondered if Bauji had always been this way, and about how his wife would have put up with him. 'Has he always been like this?' she had innocently asked Dev a few months into their marriage. 'It's just the way he is. He doesn't mean anything wrong. Don't take his words to your heart,' Dev had said fondly. From what Dev told her, not that Bauji was a very amicable person to begin with, but he had become perpetually ill-tempered after the demise of his wife. Maa, Dev's mother, had brought balance and grounding to his life. She was aware of his quirks and she knew her way around them.

More than Bauji, she was Dev's anchor—the woman who had held the Kumar household together. Renu had only heard stories of her from Dev, and every time she did, she wished Maa was still alive to guide her and be her anchor too since she came across as a strong and wise woman. Her death had taken away the purpose from Bauji's life and Dev had to switch roles from that of a son to a parent taking care of Bauji who seemed like he had given up on everything. Renu took a while to adjust to him and even though Bauji gave her moments of unpleasantness, Dev always made up for them in his own little ways. He would take her out in the evenings, or they would just stroll around in the park and talk about regular everyday things. Dev would tell her about his day at work every evening and she would talk about everything she did at home. Aneisha wasn't born yet so it was just the two of them. She wanted to work, but Dev made it clear that he wanted her to just look after the family. It wasn't the life she had imagined for herself before she married Dev, but she compromised and adjusted. Since she had spent the larger part of her youth alone, her obvious choice was to opt for the warmth and comfort of a family. *One cannot have everything*, she'd told herself every time she felt the tentacles of resentment creep up on her.

~

It was a hot and humid day in August and she was tired of going around in auto rickshaws. Dev had taken the family car with him to Sitapur. They had bought it last year on EMI, a cherry red Alto. She barely got to use the car but it made life a whole lot tougher for her. She didn't know how much her husband earned. He would just hand her Rs 15,000 on the first of every month. But now, because of the EMI, her so called 'pocket money' had been sliced down to Rs 10,000. Month after month, she struggled hard to cope with the school-related expenses, inflated prices of groceries and other bills. There were times she wished she had a career of her own—that would take care of so much. With a master's degree in geography, she knew she could have easily found a teaching job.

'Then who will take care of the kids and Bauji?' Dev had asked indignantly whenever she'd tried to discuss her job with him. Of course it was her! How could she say no? Her working meant neglecting an ageing father-in-law, growing-up kids and a house that needed constant maintenance. That was several years ago. Maybe things would get better with time, she had assured herself back then and let the topic go.

She quietly walked into the room, her hands loaded with shopping bags, and closed the door behind her. She went straight to her room. Then, pulling out a large box from one of the jute bags, she smiled, mighty pleased with herself. Inside the colourful cardboard packaging, was the remote-controlled plane that Avi had been pining for. It had cost her more than what she'd initially thought of spending but she knew Avi would be really happy receiving this on his birthday, which was next week. He wasn't a kid who would raise a fuss over a toy—this must've really meant a lot to him. She stashed it into her box-bed, which had over time, become her secret cove. Sometimes she wished she didn't have to hide mundane stuff such as this from her father-in-law but he didn't seem ready to accept her for what she was, at least not anytime soon.

She sat down on the bed with a sigh. She didn't know exactly who to blame for her mediocre life. She hadn't made this choice. In fact, she couldn't clearly remember why she had agreed to this unlikely match—her and Dev. Maybe she had too much on her mind back then to notice that Dev was nowhere close to the kind of man she had imagined herself spending the rest of her life with. He was handsome, no doubt—with dark brooding eyes and full lips. His bushy eyebrows took centre stage on his face. On their first meeting, the only one before they got married, they had gotten along just fine. He was polite, seemed well-mannered and stable; the proverbial *spark* had been there too, or so she thought at the time. It had been a few months since Dev's mother had lost her battle with cancer, and Bauji was in a hurry to get his only son married. The house was in serious need of a woman. The past few years had been a haze and she wasn't sure at which point the spark had left their relationship.

She looked around. Everything was in its place, and yet nothing was. She looked at her watch. She barely had one hour to get lunch on the table. The children would be home any minute and Bauji would start pacing up and down if his meal wasn't served on time. There was no time to feel tired; the fatigue had to be brushed aside for now. She got up and switched on the radio which she had placed in the kitchen, hoping the white noise would give her some respite.

The pressure cooker hissed in her face as she frantically chopped vegetables and tossed them into the pan. Now, to make the chapattis. Everything had to be fresh and hot.

Bauji wouldn't eat anything that had been sitting around for
long. Bringing leftovers to the table was sacrilege and was
treated like crime.

'I'm here at Global Book Store and you should see the
crowds lining up to get a copy of *First Night*!' chirped the
RJ. 'Like Maya's previous releases, this one too seems to be
a sure shot bestseller!' Renu pressed the rolling pin so hard
that it tore the chapatti in the middle. She would have to
start all over again. From the small window that connected
the kitchen to the dining room, she could see a shadow of
annoyance pass across Bauji's already disgruntled face. He
must've resented her going out and taking so long, and now
this Maya business. She just hoped he'd refrain from ranting
on the subject. She did not have the energy to listen to his
complaints about Indian culture and how every creatively
inclined person was hell-bent on destroying it.

Maya's fourth book had released today and she
wondered if Dev had got himself a copy. Should she ask
him when he came over next weekend? He was to come
over every weekend; at least that was the initial plan. And
for the first few months, he did stick to it religiously. But
then there were weekend meetings, rising fuel costs and the
long commutes. His visits trickled down to just about once
a month. She was sure he'd come the next weekend, it was
Avi's birthday after all.

~

'Maa, when is Papa going to come for my birthday party?'
asked Avinash as Renu scuttled around the house to make

arrangements. She had ordered a Spiderman cake from the neighbourhood bakery and sent out the invites to his friends. *Chhole bhature* and *dahi vada*s would surely be a hit with the little ones—they were easy to put together and not very expensive too.

'He said he'll try his best,' she said cheerfully, feeling guilty about lying to her son on his birthday. She had called Dev last night to ask what time he'd reach home.

'There is an office party. All the senior managers are coming, I have to be there,' he'd said apologetically. She'd thought she heard a woman chuckling in the background.

'Are you somewhere outside?' she'd casually asked, afraid that her interrogative tone would offend him. These days, she could never tell what would rub him the wrong way and make him angry. At times, he'd patiently answer every question she would put up but often he would just blow his lid at the slightest provocation. He wasn't anything like that when she married him. The unpredictability, the irritation and the detachment were all recent. She was slowly learning to deal with it but in the same breath, she cursed the day he had left for Sitapur. It had been a little above a year.

'No, not really . . . just watching TV,' his voice was cold and detached. The woman chuckled again.

A strange feeling of doubt and insecurity crept over Renu. She had never been the suspicious wife, but right now her instincts screamed in rebellion. *Was he with another woman?* She did not want to listen to the voice of her gut. She wanted to trust Dev. She told herself that no matter what their relationship had turned into, Dev was a simple man who would never cheat on her. And yet, it was obvious that he was rapidly drifting away from her and she seemed to be unable to do anything about it. 'Was it because of another woman that he wasn't coming home?' she wondered with a sense of dread.

Avinash would be upset about his father's absence, but the toy plane would offer some solace, she hoped. 'Beta, Papa had some urgent work so he might not be able to come. But he promised he'll make up for it when he comes next time,' she said caressing her son's soft cheeks. She had carefully timed the revelation. Avi's friends had started trickling in and she hoped that it would in some way, make up for the disappointing piece of news. Avi frowned on hearing it but as his enthused guests walked in through the doorway with gift packages in hand, he quickly forgot all about it. Renu wished she too could forget just as easily. She was glad that Dev had at least wished Avi over the phone in the morning.

FOUR

Renu was barely out of the shower when the doorbell rang. Who could it be at this early hour? The milkman had come and gone, and despite Renu's persistent harangues, the maid never came in this early. She quickly tied up her water-soaked hair in a towel and rushed outside. Bauji was sitting on the living room sofa, immersed in his newspaper, pretending to be oblivious to the sound of the doorbell. She shook her head and flung the door open. A handsome face looked back at her.

'Yes?' she said to the stranger standing in front of her. The man fished out a newspaper cutting from his pocket. He couldn't have been more than twenty-five years old.

'Good morning, I just came to enquire about a room on rent. I tried calling this number but it was switched off,' he said, pointing to the crumpled piece of paper.

'I'm sorry. You must have the wrong house. We didn't give out this ad,' she said. The towel on her head gave away, sending her thick black, waist-length hair cascading around her oval face, lighting up her complexion. The stranger smiled. His gaze made her very nervous and she put the towel on top of the shoe rack beside the door before pushing away the locks from her face. How awkward was this?

'Let him come in,' Bauji croaked from the living room. Renu moved aside to make way for the stranger. She noticed he was well-groomed, dressed in a formal blue shirt and beige trousers. He smelt nice too.

'Namaste, sir. I'm Arjun Singh Chauhan,' he bowed and folded his hands in reverence. Bauji signalled him to sit. 'I saw this ad in the paper . . .'

'Yes, yes . . .' Bauji replied and Renu's face contorted in confusion. They did have a sparsely furnished room upstairs that could be accessed from the driveway but they used it only when relatives came visiting. It heated up like a brick oven during the unbearable summers and got excruciatingly cold during winters. Aneisha, who wasn't too happy about sharing a room with her kid brother had tried making it her abode once but she was back in her old room within a couple of weeks. Now, it was being used just as a store packed with a few trunks, off-season clothes and miscellaneous objects that would never be used. Why was she not surprised that Bauji had decided to rent it out without discussing it with her? Did Dev know about this?

'Do you have a family?' Bauji started off.

'No, Bauji, I'm single,' he said casting a furtive glance in Renu's direction. She quickly turned her gaze away and made her way to the kitchen to prepare tea for this unexpected guest, who seemed like he was here to stay. She frowned at how he referred to Bauji as *bauji*, and not as *uncle* or Mr Kumar.

'Actually I run a hardware business in Kanpur. We just landed a six-month contract with a company here so I thought it will be easier if I make Lucknow my base instead of a long commute every day.' She heard him talk as she peered across the kitchen window to get a better look at him. It was much safer to observe him from the confines of the kitchen. The tea bubbled up and spilled all over the stove. Renu let out an exasperated sigh.

'Don't mind me saying this but I wouldn't prefer to rent out the place to a bachelor,' said Bauji.

'Oh! You don't have to worry about anything. I'll mind my own business, I promise.'

There was silence for a couple of minutes; Bauji seemed to be mulling over the prospect. 'The rent is Rs 4000 a month. You can cook your own food but no alcohol, partying or girls,' he said in a stern tone.

Arjun nodded in agreement. The room was perfect for a bachelor, with a tiny kitchenette in the corner and an attached bathroom. It needed a lot of cleaning though.

'Renu, get the room upstairs cleaned. This young man will be living there,' Bauji instructed Renu as she brought in the tea with some biscuits. Her mind was bustling with thoughts.

She nodded as she handed them their tea.

Arjun quickly gulped down the scalding tea. 'Thank you so much, Bauji. I have to go now or I'll be late for work. I'll bring my luggage in the evening,' he said.

'Don't you want to at least take a look at the room first?' Renu quickly blurted as he got up to leave. She wanted him to see the room the way it was, in the hope that he would reject it. Although a little extra money would be welcome, she wasn't sure how she felt about having a stranger live in their house, or giving up whatever little privacy she had living with her father-in-law.

'Oh, yes. I completely forgot!' he said with a smile looking right into Renu's eyes. She had no idea why he did that and why it made her so fidgety. *This man is trouble*, she told herself.

'Can you show it to me, please?'

Renu found herself in a fix.

'Champa will show him the room,' Bauji butted in, asking the maid, who had sauntered in by then, to accompany the gentleman.

From his face, Renu could make out that Arjun wasn't very pleased but she was secretly relieved. It would save her the awkwardness of talking to this man, at least for the time being.

It took all of five minutes for Arjun to inspect the room and give his approval, much to Renu's surprise. She knew that in its present form, the room wasn't exactly liveable.

As soon as Arjun left, Renu immediately went to her room and dialled Dev's number. 'Why didn't you tell me that you were giving the room out on rent?' she demanded as soon as he picked up the phone.

'What is wrong with it?' he answered coolly.

'Nothing wrong but you could have at least told me . . .'

'I've already discussed this with Bauji. And Renu, you are the one complaining about money and our budget all the time. I thought renting out that room will bring in some extra money, that's all. You should be happy.'

'Very well then, if you have decided to keep me out of all important decisions, so be it,' she said and hung up the phone. She was the one running the house and taking care of everything, and yet when it came to crucial discussions, nobody bothered to even ask for her opinion. It was as if she was a glorified housemaid who was not supposed to question, opine or object. This sort of a situation had become more a norm now than just a deviation. Then what was she getting so worked up about?

'Champa, we have to clean the room upstairs today. That gentleman is coming to live there,' she said with mild irritation as the maid washed the dishes in the kitchen. She now had another task which she wasn't too pleased about.

~

'Why did Dev have to do this?' she muttered under her breath as the monstrosity of the task unfolded before her. Bottles, newspapers, boxes . . . the place was a dump! As she tossed out one object after the other, it began to dawn upon her why her husband had done this—he had done this for her, or so she liked to believe. She had been complaining about money for quite some time, about sky-high prices for everything and exorbitant school fees. The children were growing up fast, and they had their own set of demands.

Some extra income, even though it wasn't much, would definitely help her cope.

Old clothes and blankets, a battered toaster, fading suitcases—Champa was all too happy to have all the old stuff to herself. Perhaps that had been the incentive for her to clean up every nook and cranny with so much sincerity, washing and scrubbing the ordinary mosaic flooring till it sparkled. Renu cleared out the cupboard and the small wooden shelf on the wall. 'How much space would a bachelor need for his belongings?' she wondered. The plumbing would need some work too.

Renu admired the beauty of the room as it emerged from under the clutter. Flanked by windows on three sides, it was spacious and airy, quite unlike the small, dingy rooms downstairs. The door opened into the terrace, which offered a panoramic view of their gated community in Indira Nagar that had a well-maintained park right in the middle of it. Pity the terrace had been reduced to a junkyard.

~

'Is he really going to live out of just two suitcases?' Renu thought as she escorted Arjun upstairs to his room that evening. She was surprised that he hadn't even bothered to look at the room carefully before agreeing to the rent. But then, he was only going to be here for a few months.

'This is your kitchen. It is small but should be enough for you,' she said pointing to the hole-in-the-wall kitchenette, 'and this is the bathroom. It doesn't have a geyser so you'll have to use the heating rod. It's in the cupboard.'

'Thank you,' he said, his eyes making direct contact with hers. She hadn't been looked at like that in a long time. And once again, she felt butterflies in her stomach.

'Let me know if you need anything,' she turned away, hiding the flush of her face.

'Sure, Renu . . .' She stopped in her tracks. Did he just call her by her first name? Not didi, bhabhiji, Mrs Kumar, but *Renu*? Should she object?

'How do you know my name?'

'Your father-in-law mentioned it when he was talking to me,' he grinned. 'I'm sorry I called you by your first name. I hope you didn't mind it.' His eyes sparkled with a hint of playfulness and remained riveted on her face.

She realized that she didn't. 'It's all right,' she said with a slight smile, unsure of what else to say. She wasn't accustomed to male attention, and certainly not of such a blatant kind. She could feel her cheeks heat up and wondered if the crimson of her face would give away her thoughts. She quickly averted her gaze from him and scuttled out of the room, her heart pounding inexplicably in her chest.

~

Renu's encounter with Arjun earlier had left her flustered. She had barely exchanged glances with this stranger and yet, he seemed to be all over her mind. Her heart lost its steady rhythm momentarily every time she recollected how he had looked at her. After a long time, she had felt something strange stir within her being. Desire for a person who was not her husband? It was strange. And scary, this incessant fluttering in her gut. She remembered that she was a middle-aged married woman and a mother of two children. How could she even allow her thoughts to stray into a territory she knew was sinful? 'NO,' she said out aloud. She wasn't going to permit these alien feelings that were germinating within her to grow. Like everything else, these too would pass, she told herself. Her eyelids grew heavy as she struggled to fight off thoughts of Arjun. It's a sin. It's a sin, she repeated to herself.

It was late in the night and silence had descended over the house at last. It was this comforting silence that always brought along with it a strange calmness for Renu. Finally, she could cast her mask aside. As she listened to the sound of her own breath, she felt all her anxieties falling away.

No one would understand how much she treasured this time, just before she fell asleep exhausted. It emboldened her. Her face suffused with warmth and a gentle smile, she could feel the familiar comfort of her bed, fitting into the contours of her curves. Her days were always lost in a numbing rush of looking after the house and everyone in it. She rarely had a minute to herself. But this silence late in the night was her shelter. Her safe place.

She had been a little more restless today than usual and had been waiting eagerly for the day to end. She pulled a soft bed sheet over herself. Her hands caressed the cool sheet as she covered herself completely with it and her hands slowly drifted under the sheet covering her. She gently tugged at her kameez and hitched it up, sliding it higher till it was bunched around her bra, and she felt the

sheet caress her bare stomach. Her mind in that moment
was a vibrant kaleidoscope of sensuality. She did not even
realize when, almost as a reflex, her fingers loosened the
knot holding her salwar up and let it slip down her legs. Her
feet wriggled a little impatiently till her salwar lay in a heap
at the foot of her bed while her other hand reached behind
and unhooked the clasp of her bra.

As she slipped out of her kameez with the slow
sensuality that always easily engulfed her alter ego—Maya—
varied images flit through her head. Dev, the anticipation
she felt on their wedding night and the early days of their
marriage. Arjun, the bold and good-looking tenant who
flirted with her shamelessly, tried to get close to her, even
complimenting her. Both of them were so different from
each other.

Her fingers slipped under her bra once they were free
from the kameez and caressed her full breasts. She liked
the weight of her ample breasts in her hands. She squeezed
one softly and let her thumb caress her nipples one by one.
She felt them turn hard under her fingers as she cupped
her palm between her legs over her panties. Her actions
were diffused, slow . . . as she enjoyed the images that filled
her mind. She pictured Dev in his usual hurried manner
of undressing them both before he took her. She'd never
really had the time to look at him properly. And she found
it difficult to hold on to a blurry image of him inside her
head. It wasn't helping her tonight.

She felt her mind involuntarily move to Arjun. She
sighed as she pictured him leaning against the wall with

that smile on his face. He was lean and muscular and he had caught her staring at him very often. She imagined how he looked without his shirt, his broad, gorgeous back as he walked across the terrace. And him reaching down to unbutton his pants to allow his manhood to spring out, leaning in on her while she boldly gazed.

The images made her warmer. Her hand involuntarily slipped into the waistband of her panties and caressed her smooth mound. She briefly hesitated before she shrugged her damp panties lower and took them off. A muffled moan escaped her lips as impatient fingers sought her eager core, her need multiplying instantly. Her head rolled back on the bed as she stroked herself. She pictured her hand reaching out and curling around his engorged throbbing hardness. Her pelvis lifted briefly off the bed as her hand fluttered faster and harder, teasing out an involuntary groan from her mouth.

She allowed her legs to thrash. The muscles inside her stomach tightened. Her hand and her fingers strummed on her nerve endings, releasing intense waves of pleasure from deep within the pit of her stomach. Inside her head, Arjun had turned her around, bent her at the waist, making her hands grab the bedposts for support as her knees trembled. When she felt him grab her waist as he thrust into her from behind, her fingers curled and set her off. She felt herself climbing a crescendo. Like a high music note. A raga playing on taut strings drawing her out further and further, her shallow breaths now making her pant, her toes curl and her chest heave as she felt the knot that had formed in the pit of her stomach explode as she climaxed. The soles of her feet rested on the bed as her pelvis lifted off the bed and her hips thrashed repeatedly against her fingers buried deep between her legs, beating a slow, hungry rhythm, till she plateaued and then began a slow descent. She trembled and shuddered, again and again, before she lowered herself into the bed slowly. She whispered his name and then pressed her sighs into her pillow and fell back in exhaustion.

Satiated but wanting.

Sleep eluded her for hours until she finally resigned herself to her usual bedtime routine—a pen and a few sheets of paper. As the words spilled over the blank white sheets, she became another woman. She became Maya.

~

'We've got to get her to come out in public, that's the only way we can save ourselves.' The woman's tone was frantic.

'But how? She never will. There's too much at stake for her.'

The woman looked at her partner, disappointment evident on her face, 'There has to be a way. There has to be some way!' She was now pacing up and down the room while the man sat hunched at the edge of the bed, his chin resting pensively over his clasped hands.

She was desperate, but he was calm, calculative. They had found the door, only the key to its lock needed to be discovered. And he knew that they couldn't be too far from it.

'Do something, will you? Or else, we're finished!' she snapped.

'Can you just shut up and sit there quietly in the corner for a while? I don't want to deal with your nagging right now.'

The woman let out an annoyed grunt and made her way to the couch, still impatient but trying hard not to distract him. There were times she wasn't happy with the way he treated her, but she knew she needed him—for everything. Whether he needed her or not, she wasn't sure, but at this stage of her life and career, she knew she could not afford to lose him.

The two sat in strained silence for a long while. She sat looking at him intermittently, fidgeting and impatient for him to say something. He barely looked in her direction. And even when he did, he seemed to be looking through her as he sat quietly, his mind in an overdrive and his face clouded with that intense concentration she had come to recognize. She knew the man sitting across the room. His silence was rarely ever futile. 'I have it. I think I have the plan,' he said in a distant, mellow voice, his chin still resting on his palms but the pensive expression had given way to a faint triumphant smirk.

FIVE

'Dev is coming today,' Bauji mumbled dryly as he ambled past the kitchen in the morning.

Renu's eyes lit up at the thought but she didn't say a word. She just slightly nodded her head instead.

'Make something nice for lunch, instead of your usual boring fare,' he growled and disappeared into the hallway.

Renu ignored his jibe; she was far too excited to even bother. She felt a spring to her step and her limbs moved faster to get past the kitchen chores. She decided to take a long leisurely bath, wash her hair, and scrub her body with a mix of *besan* and yogurt to make her skin glow. She spent some time deliberating over what to wear. Should it be a saree or a suit? It wasn't like they were going out anywhere today, but she hadn't seen Dev in weeks!

She rushed through the cooking and within an hour she had everything ready. She then dashed off to the bathroom.

God forbid, she couldn't let Dev catch her smelling of spices. She put on a simple, red-coloured suit and left her wet hair open, and then headed to the terrace to dry her hair in the sun. Arjun would have left for work by now, and she could surely use a few peaceful moments in the winter sun after the busy morning. Taking a deep breath, she settled onto a chair and gazed contently at the children playing in the park.

'Wow, you have such beautiful hair,' she heard a deep male voice from right behind her. Startled, she turned, only to find Arjun smiling at her.

'Uh . . . I . . . I thought you must be off to work by now,' she stammered, her cheeks flushing crimson yet again. His presence had a strange effect on her.

'Madam, today is Sunday, in case you forgot,' he said smugly.

'Oh yes . . . how could I . . .' she said, astounded at her own absent-mindedness. With two school-going kids, she ought to have remembered.

'That's okay. Feel right at home. It's your house after all,' he chuckled. 'You're looking gorgeous today by the way. Any special occasion?'

'Well, no actually,' Renu shifted her gaze sheepishly, unsure of where to look and how to respond. It was almost as if she had absolutely forgotten how to accept any compliments from men. But then, it had been a long while since anyone complimented her, especially for how she looked. She blurted out an awkward 'Thanks', feeling like her face was on fire.

What exactly is the matter with this man? Where she lived, men didn't dole out compliments to unfamiliar women just like that.

'I'm sorry if my comment made you uncomfortable,' he said in an earnest voice as Renu shifted around on her feet. She realized that she should probably ignore him or snub him by making her displeasure known, then why was she struggling to find her voice in front of this man who was several years younger than her?

'Never mind that,' he continued. 'Let me get you some tea. It is a nice sunny day to sit on the terrace with a cup of chai, no?'

'No, no. Please don't bother. I was about to go downstairs anyway; there are a million things to do.'

'The million things can wait . . .'

She discovered, much to her surprise, that she was actually *enjoying* his attention, and his company. As Arjun turned around to walk towards the door of his room, Renu caught herself soaking in his broad shoulders that tapered down to his waist in a masculine curve. And that pert posterior; she hadn't seen one like that outside of the television screen. She quickly shook her head and wrapped her arms around her body, as if to protect herself from this sudden, flickering spark of forbidden desires.

It took all of five minutes for Arjun to emerge with two steaming cups of tea in his hands. He handed one over to Renu with a smile and she smiled back in return. As much as she loved the beverage, she couldn't remember the last time someone had served her tea as she sat soaking up the winter sun. In fact, on most days, she could barely steal a few moments to relish her morning cup of chai, before hurrying back to get the children ready for school and attending to Bauji, who mostly sat in the living room rattling off orders.

She lifted the cup to her lips and slowly took in the aroma emanating from it. The sun shone bright but the air was still cold, and the first sip warmed her insides like never before. Never had tea tasted so good. Was it just the tea? Why hadn't she thought of bringing her cup up on the terrace earlier? Maybe she ought to make a routine of it . . .

'I hope the sugar is all right?' Arjun's voice snapped her out of her reveries.

'It's perfect! Thank you so much. It feels really good,' she replied, surprised at the chirpiness in her own voice. The two sat on the old plastic garden chairs and Arjun allowed her a few moments of silence as she savoured the tea. A strange yet pleasant heaviness engulfed her as the steaming, syrupy tea made its way down her throat. Every time she made loud slurping noises and then let out an audible exhale, his lips broke into a smile, but he was careful not to let his amusement show.

'You don't look like someone who could make such decent chai,' she finally said, looking into her now half-empty cup.

'So what do people who can make a cup of decent chai look like?' he raised his eyebrows mockingly.

'I mean, bachelors like you don't really know their way around the kitchen, do they?' her eyes shone with mischief and the corners of her full mouth curled into a delicate smirk.

'Madam, don't be too quick to judge! I can cook a lot more than you can imagine!' he retaliated.

'I don't believe you!'

'If you want me to prove my culinary skills, have dinner with me, here at my house,' he said grinning like a schoolboy.

Renu threw her head back and laughed. As tempting as that sounded, she also knew how impractical it was. She couldn't possibly come up here to a strange man's room and have dinner with him. She couldn't possibly . . .

In between all the chatter, the thoughts of Dev arriving home had all but disappeared from her mind. It was the honking of Dev's car at the gate that finally snapped her out of her thoughts.

'Okay, listen, I have to go. Dev is here. Have to get the children dressed.' She got up from the chair and ran her fingers through her damp hair, just to get that last bit of sun into them before she went down to a cold, tube-lit house. 'Thank you for the tea. It was lovely!'

'You really miss him, huh?' Arjun called after her as she strode towards the door leading to the staircase. Renu paused in her step and turned to look at him. She could not fathom what exactly his eyes were trying to say to her at that moment. She had barely known him for a few days but she had already felt those eyes speaking to her and saying things his words didn't, and she was scared to delve deep within her to discover their meaning.

'It doesn't matter,' she said softly, and went downstairs.

SIX

Renu's heart trembled a little as Dev's car pulled into the driveway. She soon realized, quite ruefully, that the tremors she felt with him being physically present with her were nothing like the passionate tingles she felt when she was alone with thoughts of him inside her head. The ones she was feeling right now were more a result of nervousness and anxiety and trepidation—not of the good kind.

Dev stepped out of the car and dove straight to touch Bauji's feet, while Renu stood on the other side. She forced out a half-smile when Dev turned his gaze towards her, and nodded in acknowledgement. She hovered around him as he unpacked his bags in their room, as one would do with a first-time guest, to make sure he was comfortable and had everything he needed. When the maid brought in a glass of water on a tray, she took it from her hands and went on to hand it over to her husband herself.

'Thanks,' Dev muttered as he picked up the glass and drank from it.

'Dev . . .' her voice choked a little but she had rehearsed this so many times, over and over again. She could no longer ignore the elephant in the room; she had to talk to Dev and there was no better time than now.

'What?' he asked, still not making eye contact with her.

'I . . . I . . . need to discuss something with you . . .' she blurted after a lot of deliberation. This was not going to be easy. *Talking things out* had been a concept alien to her, until she had read about it in magazines and self-help books. But for all the difficulty it posed before her, she knew it was the only shot she had at leading a normal married life.

'About what?'

'About us . . . about our marriage . . .'

Dev let out a long exhausted sigh. 'Renu, I have just come home after a long tiring drive and you want to have this useless discussion right now?' His tone wasn't loud, accusatory, or even borderline rude—just blunt and matter-of-fact.

Useless. Of course, it was going to be useless! Maybe it was time to come to terms with the fact that nothing spectacular or even moderately pleasant was ever going to come out of any conversation with him. He was always going to be cold, distant and detached; totally oblivious to her loneliness and pining. He would ask after the kids, have his meals, watch some TV and then roll over to sleep.

'I'm sorry. I shouldn't have . . .' she said. Her nervousness had ebbed away to a distance where she could no longer feel it and a deep, nagging pain had taken its place. 'I'll just go and prepare lunch.'

Renu walked over to the kitchen and just stood there. She had already cooked everything in the morning, but being in the same room as him felt strangely uncomfortable and awkward. She had never felt this before but something about his aura stifled her now.

But Dev was her husband and the father of her children. She had to make it work, at least for their sake. She would look for another opportunity to talk to him, she decided. It had to be done.

As she laid out lunch on the table, Dev stepped out of the room, all showered and dressed.

'I have to meet some friends for lunch and then some others in the evening. Will come home late. Don't wait up,' he announced to no one in particular and made his way out of the door.

'All right,' said Bauji coolly and adjusted himself into the chair waiting to be served, but Renu's mind was somewhere else. A mish-mash of thoughts erupted in her brain and her eyes welled up with rage and frustration.

'Maa, I'll take care of it,' Aneisha said, instinctively sensing her mother's pain, and took the ladle from Renu's hand.

Without saying a word, Renu rushed into her room and buried her face in the pillows, to muffle out the noise her cries were about to make. Then after she had cried out, she lay still and alone in her bed all afternoon, blank-faced and stony-eyed. For the first time in her life, she wished Dev hadn't come home. The thought instantly filled her with guilt. *What kind of a wife thinks like that?* As she grappled with the uncontrollable deluge of emotions, Aneisha walked in on her.

'You okay, Maa?' asked the sixteen-year-old hesitantly, placing a gentle hand on her mother's shoulder.

'Nothing, beta, I'm fine,' said Renu, forcing her lips into a smile. She knew her daughter was very perceptive, but she wasn't yet ready to be subjected to the convoluted mess that her life had become. And she thought, young girls like her daughter should be immersing themselves in fairy tales, not listening to sordid details of an ageing woman's broken heart.

'Let's go upstairs for a while, Maa. You will feel better,' offered Aneisha cheerfully. Renu was glad her daughter respected her silence and did not ask any more questions.

The two climbed up to the terrace and indeed, the pleasant evening breeze and the vermillion-streaked sky lifted some weight off her chest, albeit temporarily.

'You know, Maa, our physics teacher got called to the principal's office today.'

'Why so?'

'He was caught playing games on his phone during the assembly!' Aneisha burst into giggles. Renu couldn't contain her smile despite her inner turmoil. She put an arm around her daughter and hugged her tight. 'Isn't it time for your tuition class?'

'I think I'll skip it today. I've already studied the chapter they are going to cover,' said Aneisha.

'No, Aneisha, this is not right. You should not miss any classes, you know that,' explained Renu. She knew Aneisha was lying.

'But, Mom!'

'Aneisha, I am a grown-up person. I can take care of myself,' she smiled and assured her daughter, holding her by the shoulders and looking into her eyes. Aneisha nodded with scepticism, but then quietly made her way downstairs to collect her books. Renu smiled fondly and shook her head after her—these kids were all she had, and she would do anything to protect them and to give them a secure future, even if it meant sacrificing her own happiness. She hadn't wanted Aneisha to grow up so fast but she knew her daughter was an intuitive child. There was no way she could shield her from the realities of her life and their family for too long.

While she rued Aneisha's quickly fading innocence, a part of her was glad to have someone who understood and supported her like an adult. Aneisha was no longer a child dependent on her mother for everything—she was a wise young girl who absorbed everything around her like a sponge and understood the circumstances even if she did not voice her opinion loudly yet. Renu promised herself again that unlike her own mother, she would always have her daughter's back.

'I thought you would be busy with your husband today.'

Renu turned around in surprise to find Arjun standing behind her. She cursed herself under her breath. Why did she always forget that this terrace was no longer her exclusive territory? She stared at him unblinkingly for a moment, paralysed, not knowing what she should say in return. She felt a little guilty for impinging upon their tenant's privacy every now and then and also a little embarrassed for putting herself in the situation so often lately.

'I'm really sorry. I keep coming upstairs without realizing . . .' she blurted out.

'You don't have to be sorry. In fact, I should be thanking you for letting me have the pleasure of your company,' said Arjun in his customary deep, charming voice that again made Renu blush for a second and look away from him.

'How the hell does he get me feeling like this every single time?'
'Tea?'

Renu burst out laughing. This was the second time in the day Arjun was about to make tea for her, and his kind gesture took away a large chunk of her stress and warmed up her heart. I should come here more often, she thought to herself.

And just like that, all her pain and heaviness faded into thin smoke, at least for a while. She was soon smiling, laughing and chatting with her newfound friend.

'So where is the mister? Haven't seen him around . . .' asked Arjun and Renu's smile withered at the mention of her husband.

'He's gone out somewhere . . . for work,' she replied shortly, trying hard to camouflage her discomfort at defending him unsuccessfully.

'Ah, okay. I thought you might have scared him away with your long, black hair . . .' he grinned.

'Oh dear, there you go again,' said Renu, rolling her eyes, 'You know compliments make me really uncomfortable, but thank you!'

'Sorry, didn't mean to make you feel uncomfortable.' There was an inexplicable intensity in Arjun's eyes, and it was amazing how he could switch between being irresistibly charming and innocently boyish within no time. There was something about him that set him apart from others, but it was something Renu couldn't quite put a finger on.

'Never mind that. I think I should go . . .' Renu snapped, extremely unsure of where this conversation was heading. She was a tad uncomfortable, but also curious; she felt like a gawky, awkward teenager who had just discovered the joy of being admired by the opposite sex.

'I am sure you must be getting lots of compliments from men all the time. Must be tough to react to those every time. Isn't it?'

'No, I don't actually,' she said coyly. *Was he flirting with her? Why would a young, handsome man like himself shower so much attention on a middle-aged housewife like her? And what the hell was wrong with her? Why was she unable to stop him from saying these cheesy things and herself from enjoying them?*

'Maybe they are just scared of your beauty. I think you are really gorgeous. You have lovely hair and your voice is pure music.'

'Stop, please just stop,' Renu struggled hard to hold back the giggles erupting in her stomach but ultimately burst out laughing at Arjun's childlike persistence.

'Sorry, just can't help it. I need to answer god when he questions me about what did I do when I spotted such a spellbindingly beautiful woman!'

'You are just too much, Arjun! How do you even come up with such filmy dialogues! How many women have you practised these lines on?'

'You break my heart, milady. Trust me, all those words pour forth right from the deepest corners of my soul,' Arjun replied with comically exaggerated indignation, holding her gaze. For a moment, she found herself lost in his deep, dark eyes and almost believed him. Her throat felt strangely dry and she gulped nervously.

'Your husband has to be the luckiest man alive.'

'Shut up, Arjun' Renu laughed and lifted her arm to smack him at the back of his head playfully, but he ducked and her finger poked his eye.

'Ow,' he yelled like a child.

'I am so sorry!' she cried, rushing to check if she hadn't accidentally punctured his eyeball. 'I'm really sorry,' she repeated. 'Let me take a look!'

Arjun thrust his face forward and Renu instinctively blew warm air into the *pallu* of her cotton saree and began dabbing it on his left eye.

'Ahh, suddenly it feels better,' he croaked.

His were the most beautiful pair of ebony eyeballs she had ever gazed into and she found it difficult to keep her attention on the task at hand. A bushy cluster of raven-black lashes sprang wildly from the edges of his eyes, much like a tropical flower in full bloom.

She quickly stepped away, guilt coursing through every nerve in her body.

'It still hurts,' he said, sounding like a whiny kid with a deep baritone.

His mischievous smirk told her that he was just fooling around now, but she found herself struggling against her desire to oblige him.

'I don't dole out free treatment like that,' she finally said haughtily. Her tone had a hint of naughtiness to it and her grin, more so. The sun had set a while ago and his thick stubble gleamed as he bent forward and came in the way of a gentle, yellow beam from the streetlight. Renu took a moment to marvel as the light framed his magnificent features and bounced off his edgy jawline.

She was now standing too close to him, within breathing distance.

'You have beautiful eyes,' her dusky complexion turned a fiery red as he whispered those words, not so playfully any more. She suddenly felt conscious of their physical proximity and her heart fluttered like a crazy butterfly, like a young fledgling about to take its maiden flight.

As she leaned closer for another feeble attempt at soothing his eye, she felt the tip of his nose lightly brush against her breast. A delicious spasm coursed through her body and she closed her eyes to savour the moment in its entirety, hoping silently that she was the only one who could feel it.

A month later, her marriage to Dev would complete nineteen years and her celibacy, almost an entire year. She had exercised great self-control far too long and had gotten really good at it, yet she couldn't ignore the ache between her legs that reared its head at the most inopportune moments—like right now.

Her mind resisted but her body involuntarily drew itself closer to him, until her face was half-buried in his raven-black hair. He didn't seem to mind the proximity. Rather, he let his fingers creep gently along her waist and nuzzled further in, unfazed by her nervously heaving bosom. Her breathing grew shallow and strange tingles took over every inch of her being, numbing her better sense. She leaned back deliriously and almost lost her balance before he held her by her bare waist. She tried to pull back reluctantly from the hypnosis she found herself in and kicked over the plastic chair lying just behind her. The sudden noise broke the trance and brought her back to reality from her deliriously intoxicated state.

'NO! This is not right!' she yelled and jerked her rebellious body away from his as tears welled up in her eyes.

'I'm sorry! I didn't mean to do that. I am extremely sorry, Renu. Believe me, it just happened. I had no idea what I was doing,' said Arjun as he ran his fingers through his hair in an attempt to make sense of the situation and gain back his composure. But before he could even complete his sentence, Renu bolted.

She scurried down to her room and locked the door behind her, breathing heavily to calm down the frenzied thing pounding in her chest. She was in a daze. Her mind seemed to be strangely disconnected with her body. She could understand perfectly, yet not understand at all what was happening. She stared with disbelief at her dishevelled hair and flushed face in the mirror with a blank stare, at her face which had a strange glow of the kind she hadn't seen on herself in years, the glow she thought she was incapable of feeling any more. The scent of Arjun's cologne seemed to be smeared all over her, and she realized that it was emanating from her clothes.

'Renu! What the hell are you doing? This is so bloody wrong!' she cried out to herself. 'Dev will never forgive you if he finds out!'

And yet, she couldn't bring herself to feel as guilty as she thought she ought to have felt as an erring wife. A loud knock on the door jolted her out of her chaotic thoughts, and she opened it to find Dev standing there.

'How come you are back so early?' she blurted, instantly noticing the accusatory tone in her own words. 'I mean . . . you said . . .' she looked up at the wall clock and saw it was almost eleven in the night. She had lost all sense of the passage of time.

Dev raised an eyebrow, unable to fathom his wife's unusual reaction. 'I thought you would be happy to see me,' he retorted sarcastically.

'Of course, I am. Why wouldn't I be? I hope you enjoyed the evening with your friends!' Renu replied in a flustered voice, which had a strange, fake enthusiastic pitch that belied what she was actually feeling within. She hoped fervently that unlike her, at least Dev wouldn't notice it.

'Yes, I did,' Dev nodded sceptically. Wasn't his wife always the one to sulk whenever he spent an evening out by himself? *'I hope you enjoyed the evening with your friends!'* What on earth had gotten into her?

Dev changed into his night suit and climbed into bed.

'Dev, if you are not too tired, I want to talk.'

'Please, Renu, not now,' he cut her short abruptly and turned away from her to sleep. This time, however, she wasn't about to give up on him so easily. She grasped him by the shoulder and turned him around until his eyes met hers.

'What is it, Renu? Can't you see I'm tired?' he snapped.

'I'm tired too, Dev. I'm tired of waiting for you. I'm tired of your indifference! I'm tired being a nobody in your life!' Renu had meant to say all of this calmly, and strongly, but she couldn't contain the hot gush of tears from streaming down her flushed face.

Dev dragged himself up and propped himself against the pillow. 'Great. That's just great. Now you are crying too. What the hell is wrong with you? Can I have some peace in my own house if you'd permit it, please?' he said in a low hissing voice that was devoid of any affection or even politeness, for that matter.

'You tell me!' she retaliated. 'What is wrong with me that you don't want to spend even a moment in my company? What exactly is wrong with me that you run away from home at the slightest excuse? What is wrong with me that you don't even want to touch me any more? I am your wife for heaven's sake, Dev!'

'Oh, I get it now. So this is what it is all about, eh?' retorted Dev, turning his gaze away from her and looking into the far corner of the room as if in deep thought. Renu paused to take a breath and reached out for the bottle of water on the nightstand. She had said whatever she had to say. It was now up to Dev to iron out the kinks in their marriage. The ball was in his court. Renu closed her eyes and took several deep breaths in an attempt to calm herself down, hoping that Dev would apologize for his hurtful attitude, or at least be man enough to acknowledge it.

Dev didn't utter a word but instead got up from the bed, pulled down his pyjamas and threw himself upon Renu without a warning. 'This is what you want, right?' he said angrily, as his hands groped between the folds of her saree, even as she squirmed with humiliation. Yes, she wanted him to be intimate with her, but not like this. Not with so much bitterness and spite. Not as if he was doing her a favour out of charity. Before her already numb brain could decide whether to push him away or give in to him, he had already forced himself inside her and in moments, rather seconds, he was done.

'There. That makes you happy now?' Dev hissed viciously as Renu lay on the bed, frozen with angst and disgust, feeling deeply violated. 'Is there anything else you want to talk about or was that it?'

'Thanks a lot, Dev. I think I've got all my answers now,' Renu whispered bitterly after a few moments, but Dev had already turned away to his side, facing away from her.

Sleep eluded her for the rest of the night, and she just lay on the bed, blankly staring at the ceiling fan whirring above her head while Dev snored right next to her. She knew this was the beginning of the end and strangely, she hardly felt any pain at the prospect of going away from Dev. Something had finally died that night, something that had started withering and festering inside her since she wasn't sure when, and she didn't even have an opportunity to mourn its loss because she was too caught up in her dreary mind-numbing reality and also because she thought that if she did not acknowledge it, then it perhaps had a chance to come back to life somehow. She realized that night that perhaps it was her love for Dev.

~

All of next morning, she wasn't quite where she was supposed to be. She went about her daily chores mechanically but today, she felt less of her own self present in the house, lesser than what she usually felt. Her innards felt hollow and drained, and despite the sunny day outside, all she could see and feel was gloomy darkness engulfing her soul. She didn't respond when Aneisha and Avi waved her goodbye from the gate before boarding the school bus, and neither did she hear Bauji when he asked her to fetch her breakfast. She felt like she was having an out-of-body experience, her soul completely detached from her physical self. Her body was in the house physically, but it felt like she was watching it from a distance. Watching herself play one role after another as the clock went round incessantly in circles every day, all roles except her true self. What was her true self, anyway? This fantasy world she had built in her mind? Or this life of domesticity that she could not get out of?

In moments like these, her thoughts always went back to her childhood, her first brush with loneliness. She had never truly experienced the warmth of a family, and she'd thought she'd find that with Dev when she met him the first time. Family. Love. Warmth. Comfort. Sure, they'd had their moments as a couple but after all the years of giving everything and receiving little in return, she felt lost and alone and cheated. Dev seemed to have drifted far away from her; he barely showed any interest in her as a woman. Apart from their children, they had little left in common now. At times, all Renu yearned for was companionship, someone to talk to, someone to listen, someone who'd understand, someone who she could have a real conversation with. And Dev had turned out to be none of those.

SEVEN

Dear Maya,

Hope you are doing well. I am pleased to inform you that First Night has sold over 50,000 copies within the first month of its release! Congratulations! I am already eagerly awaiting your next manuscript, which, I'm sure, will be a bigger hit.

As we discussed over the phone the other day, I have some paperwork to go through with you. May I request you to drop in at our office, since you've asked us not to send any correspondence to your residence? I understand it may be slightly difficult for you to make time from your busy day at home, but I would not have bothered you if it wasn't urgent.

Maybe we could grab a cup of coffee? It's been a while since we met.

Cheers,
Akriti
Commissioning Editor
Ravenhouse Publishers Pvt. Ltd

Renu's heart skipped a beat. Akriti was the only person apart from her who knew Maya's true identity. When Ravenhouse had offered Renu a contract for the first time, nobody knew who she was, and she never had the courage to reveal herself either. All her correspondence got delivered to a box at the post office and she had a separate email ID for all her communication with the editors and the accounts department of the publishing house. However, working together had brought Akriti and Renu close as individuals too, and one day, in a fleeting moment of faith, Renu had decided to let Akriti in on her biggest secret. Even though it was long ago, she clearly remembered the day when she got her first email from Akriti. She was then a young editor who was assigned Renu's first manuscript. It was a first for both of them and at that point, nervousness was the only thing they had in common. Renu credited Akriti for a large part of her success and Akriti took pride in being 'Maya's editor'. When it came to their respective professions, the two women had practically grown together, nudging and egging each other on.

'I would really like to meet you,' Renu had said one day, without giving it much thought.

'Are you sure?' Akriti had asked. She was well-acquainted with Maya the writer but strangely oblivious to the woman behind that name.

They had fixed a day and time to meet.

'Oh, you are exactly the opposite of what I'd imagined you to be!' Akriti had exclaimed when she saw Renu sitting in the coffee shop waiting for her. Her bemused expression had only made Renu laugh. Of course, she was nowhere close to what her words made her out to be. She was not only a far cry from Maya, but quite an antithesis.

'Are you disappointed?' Renu had asked Akriti.

'Not at all, fascinated actually,' the latter had replied. And that was the beginning of a long friendship between the unlikeliest of souls.

The confession didn't come without its fair share of fear and anxiety but Renu had never regretted it. If anything, it had been liberating and Akriti had kept up her end of the trust the two women shared.

She looked out of the window at the greying sky and the little droplets of water trickling down the windowpane. Dev had already left early in the morning, the kids had been packed off to school in their raincoats and Bauji had been fed breakfast and given his multiple doses of morning tea. Last night's events had left Renu with a bitter feeling, but that email from Akriti brought about a feeble smile on her face. At least *something* was going right in her life! She remembered the day when she had very hesitantly submitted one of her pieces for a short-story competition organized by Ravenhouse Publishers a few years ago. Much to her surprise, her story had bagged the first prize and made its way to an anthology. Akriti, the editor, was the one who had then egged her to write more. 'Your writing has a rare spark. You really should write a book!' she had exhorted, but Renu did not believe her then. It was only when she had held the first royalty cheque in her hands that she half believed reluctantly that this was something she could actually be good at, and that despite her mundane boring life, she too could have something to call her own. So what if she could never publicly lay claim to it.

Renu quickly changed out of her nightie and pulled out an umbrella from a shelf next to the main door. Just as she was about to hail an auto from the street, she stopped briefly in her tracks. Bauji. She hadn't informed Bauji! She turned to walk back to the house, thinking of which excuse to deploy this time. School fees? Groceries? Renu stood still under the gentle drizzle contemplating her next move. What will he say? Will he get angry, as usual?

'Oh what the heck,' Renu muttered to herself and stuck her hand out to the first auto that came by. She would deal with the cranky old man when she got back. Or maybe she wouldn't deal with him at all! She would just make herself some tea, lock herself up in her room and turn up the volume of the television to drown out his unending nagging.

'Renu, what has gotten into you?' she questioned herself as the auto bounced over uneven roads leading up to her destination. The office of Ravenhouse Publishers was in the heart of Hazratganj and Renu longingly looked at the shops and restaurants where she had spent many a leisurely evening with her friends as a college student. Awadh Girls' Degree College was hardly a distance away from this bustling marketplace and it was a kind of routine for her gang of girls to drop by after classes for a snack and indulge in some window shopping before heading home. Oh, how long it had been since she had seen any of them! Those days seemed to have lost themselves in the grimy pages of history, and they seemed so far, far away when she tried to fish them out from the recesses of her mind.

~

'Is she coming?' demanded the man standing at the edge of the door of Akriti's office. His voice was low, but authoritative.

'Yes, sir. I mailed her this morning. And she's just called to confirm. She should be here any moment,' Akriti replied, standing up from her chair. It seemed like he was going to say something but then stopped in his tracks. It wasn't usual for her boss to come down to her office. In fact, she rarely saw him around.

'Is there anything I can help you with, sir?' she asked politely. The pensive expression on the man's face perturbed her and gave her a strange vibe. She could sense something was wrong but couldn't quite figure out what.

~

The office building opened into a narrow by-lane in Halwasia, tucked inconspicuously amidst busy shops thronged by people at all hours of the day. Renu carefully looked all around to escape any familiar faces before she stepped into the premises of Ravenhouse. She had been here only once in the past, to sign her five-book contract right after her first book turned out to be a bestseller. It had been two years since then and she only vaguely remembered the tiny cabin at the far end of the corridor that was Akriti's office.

'Renu! It is so nice to see you!' chirped Akriti as Renu walked into her office after a hesitant knock on the frosted glass door.

Ravenhouse wasn't one of the publishing biggies but they had benefitted hugely from Maya's popularity. As for Renu, she was both happy and relieved to meet Akriti. They talked on the phone quite often, but there was something very comforting about meeting someone face-to-face outside of the Kumar household. It wasn't often that she got to step out of the house, unless there was an errand to be run. Her trips had been more frequent ever since Dev left for Sitapur, since the entire responsibility of the house now rested on her. She had no dearth of reasons to go out for, but she really had nowhere to go. For many years now, her life and her world had mostly been confined to the boundaries of her home, family and her children.

Renu's thoughts briefly went back to Arjun who had been her only real contact with the outside world, albeit only fleetingly. *I have to stop crossing his path,* she reminded herself sternly. Renu hadn't been too conscious of the gradual depletion of relationships from her life since her marriage to Dev. She hardly had a family to speak of, and her friends from college had probably found it hard to keep up with a woman who could barely spare a few minutes of a day for herself.

Looking after Bauji, Dev and the household had sucked up all her life force, so much so that she now had nothing to call solely her own, not even her identity. In retrospect, it now seemed to be a worthless investment. But at least she had her children. Renu smiled at the thought. And they made every sacrifice she had made worth it.

'Arré, what happened? Why are you so lost?' chirped Akriti and snapped Renu out of her delirium as both of them walked into the coffee shop.

'I'm sorry Akriti. I just . . . oh, never mind!' Renu said with a bright smile as she hugged Akriti briefly and settled into a chair.

They caught up about how their lives were going, ordered coffee and then Akriti got to the point. 'Your books are doing very well, Renu, but we feel there's a monotony creeping in. Is everything all right with you? Are you able to give enough time to your writing, Renu?' Akriti asked, as she handed over a thin bundle of papers to Renu. They were her contracts.

'That maybe because there have been just too many things going on lately,' Renu answered. 'But I can definitely do better, Akriti. We can discuss any points that you might have. But I do want to thank you for your continued faith in me.'

Renu barely skimmed through the sheaf of papers before signing at the bottom of each. She trusted Akriti and she really didn't care for the fine print, as long as she got to write what she wanted and her books were being published. That they were so popular and loved by her readers, was an added blessing. Akriti's words did not sound pleasant but Renu knew that Akriti was not wrong. Her loyal readers only needed her name on the cover of the book to make a purchase, but as a writer she knew something was fading. Her passion for writing was in the right place but inspiration had left her side somewhere along the way. Her writing needed a new spark.

By the time their coffees arrived, they were finished with their business discussions and talking more about the writing and ideas going forward. Once finished, Akriti suggested they walk back to the Ravenhouse Publishers' office. 'And now that you are here, you might as well collect your cheque too, in person,' Akriti said with a smile.

Renu smiled uneasily. It wasn't easy for her to go to the bank time and again to manage her finances because she couldn't afford to plant any doubts in Bauji's head. However, that day it worked out all right since she could drop the cheque at her bank on the way back. She would take any chance that life would offer her.

EIGHT

It wasn't typical of Renu to take detours while she was out on errands, at least not until now. But ever since she had met Arjun, she seemed to be sprouting little wings of her own. She was supposed to buy groceries but she let herself stray into a bookstore instead. It was only when the heavenly smell of freshly printed paper filled up her nostrils, that she realized what small sensory pleasures she had been depriving herself of all these years. She spotted her books neatly arranged in the top row of a shelf right next to the entrance among other bestsellers and she couldn't resist running her fingers fondly over them.

More than pride, seeing her labours of love there gave her a sense of solace, and a deep satisfaction of having something she could call hers, and hers alone. She took her time browsing through the shelves and picked out a bunch of books that she'd been wanting to read. It had been way too long since she had treated herself to brand-new books. Most of her indulgences came from the small bookstore that stocked used books near her house, because at one time, that's all she was able to afford for herself.

'Looking for something?' asked a deep voice from behind her.

Startled, she turned. 'What are you doing here?' Renu asked, a strange knot forming in the pit of her stomach on seeing Arjun standing beside her. Creeping up behind her and then startling her with his gorgeous voice had somehow become his trademark style.

'I could ask you the same thing,' he replied. He looked exceptionally handsome even in his striped shirt and gaberdines.

'I . . . I . . . just came to buy some stuff for the children,' she stammered, looking away.

'Nice. Come, let's have coffee,' he offered.

'No, thank you. I am not much of a coffee person and I don't think it is a good idea anyway,' she replied curtly, remembering their last meeting. Did he not remember any of that or was he just pretending that it never happened?

'Why so?' he asked with an innocent face.

'Are you mad! Here? What if someone sees us together?' It was one of those rare times when her own words shocked her. There was a certain thrill in this clandestine meeting that seemed so wrong by all conventional measures of logic.

'Nothing will happen, trust me!' he said confidently.

Renu couldn't refuse but she was surprised at her own reaction. Even though she hadn't said anything overtly, she knew that her equation with Arjun was heading into dangerous waters. She had waddled at the shallow end all her life, and now she found it hard to resist the dark unknown depths that beckoned her.

They slipped into a quaint coffee shop teeming mostly with young college-goers. Renu had barely begun flipping through the menu when a largish brownie arrived at their table, with a tiny candle stuck in its succulent middle.

'Excuse me, we haven't . . .'

'Happy birthday, Renu!' Arjun cut her short as he signalled the waiter to leave.

Renu sat stunned into silence. It was her birthday. Of course, it was her birthday! How could she have forgotten? Then again how could she not have? It had been years since anything eventful had happened on her birthday. In fact, she doubted if anyone at home even remembered it. Yes, Aneisha would always wish her first thing in the morning, even if everybody else, including Renu, forgot. But she had an exam today, so perhaps it had slipped her mind. She remembered her first birthday after her marriage to Dev—he had bought her a jewellery box and they had gone out for dinner to a local Chinese restaurant. Dev wasn't very fond of Chinese food, but he knew Renu liked it and he did his bit to make the day special for her. In fact, he had done that for quite a few years, at least until Avi was born. Life since then had become a mundane vortex of predictability. Renu immersed herself in her home and motherhood and Dev worked all the time to provide for the growing family. Somewhere in the

midst of all this domesticity, the colours faded from their
lives. The moments of togetherness dwindled, words grew
scarcer and distances grew.

'Th . . . th . . . thanks. I really don't know what to say.
How did you know?' Renu blurted out, visibly flustered
and a little more than embarrassed.

'I do my research on people I care about,' Arjun said,
his lips curling into a lopsided smile.

'What does that mean?' The tension in her lips told her
that she was enjoying this, and she didn't want it to end.

'That's not important. Moreover, I live in your house.
So let's just say I chanced upon the information and it was
a coincidence that I bumped into you here! Now cut this
damn brownie, will you? I'm really hungry!'

Renu held back her giggles and ran the cheap plastic
knife through the gooey cake. She lifted a small piece and
held it before Arjun's lips. He gladly obliged.

'Excuse me, can we have some tissues please?' she called
out to the waiter.

'That won't be necessary,' said Arjun softly as he
delicately licked the chocolate icing off her fingers, sending
hot currents searing through her body. She suddenly wished
there was no one else in the cafe. Oh, how she wished he
would move beyond her fingers.

'Your turn now,' said Arjun, snapping her out of her
rapture. Renu looked at the piece of cake in his hands and
with trembling lips, took a little bite.

'Looks like we are going to need tissues after all,' said
Arjun, in mock disappointment, but before he could call

for the waiter, Renu took his hand in hers and one by one, plunged his fingers deep into her mouth.

Oh god, this was wrong. So wrong! But why did it feel so right? She hadn't felt so desired ever in her life. And so liberated! It was as if, in Arjun's company, she was an entirely different woman. Not a dull unappreciated housewife burdened with chores. Not a mother, not a wife and not a daughter-in-law. With Arjun she felt like a goddess, a woman to be desired, loved and pined after. A seductress. With Arjun she was free, she felt she was her true self. Truly Maya.

NINE

There was an unusual bounce to her step when Renu entered the house that afternoon. There was still some time left for the children to come back home, just enough for her to change and get lunch ready. Normally, she would have finished off all the cooking in the morning but this particular morning had been frantic. She remembered that she hadn't even informed Bauji before leaving the house and she knew she would have to answer for it, but she wasn't the least bit worried.

Sure enough, as she was hurriedly chopping vegetables, Bauji sauntered into the living room. 'Where had you vanished?' he asked in an annoyed tone. He would never scream or yell at her but something about his tone always reeked of authority; like he not only owned the house, but also the people living in it.

'A friend had fallen very sick suddenly. She needed someone to go with her to the hospital so I had to leave urgently. It was very crowded there today, Bauji. We had to wait for a long time.'

Bauji didn't look very convinced. 'Doesn't she have family members to take care of these things?'

'Her husband is out of town. There was no one at home. And moreover, Bauji, you always say this is how society works. Today if we help someone, tomorrow they may do the same for us,' Renu replied with a smile. Bauji nodded reluctantly. She had never had the courage to step out of her boundaries without permission from Dev or Bauji, let alone lie to them. And strangely enough, she didn't feel the slightest tinge of guilt today.

Later that afternoon, after the children had come home and wished her with handmade cards, she'd served them their lunch and talked about the papers. Then they had gone to their room to rest and prepare for the next day's exam. Renu got the opportunity to look back at what had happened earlier that day. Arjun had been knocking at the dusty corners of her soul ever since she had first seen him. Every time she was alone, he seemed to take over her imagination completely. Her heart raced at the memory of him licking the chocolate icing off her fingers and the mischievous glint in his eyes when he looked at her. She didn't know much about him yet, who he was and where he came from, but there was something extremely compelling about him. Despite his frivolous boyish banter, his words touched her deep and even the slightest accidental brush of his fingers on her skin sent her into a tizzy.

Renu, however, was no nubile teenager. She was aware of her intense attraction towards this man but at the same time, she was also curious about him. From what it appeared, their casual conversations were growing by the day and they seemed to be moving into some strange direction. She tried to ask herself what it was. Where was it headed? Then she told herself that it was perhaps too early for any kind of conjectures. It was just a chance date at a coffee shop and maybe she had given in to a moment of flirtation. What could possibly go wrong there? At the same time, she couldn't deny the explosive chemistry she felt between Arjun and herself. It was so palpable that it felt like it had teased awake every cell in her body. He was slowly making inroads into her mind, her heart and her fantasies, and that scared her a lot.

She suddenly realized that she hadn't called Dev for a while. She had hoped that he'd call her on her birthday at least, but the entire day had passed without so much as a message from him. She had grown used to this over the years, but that did not stop her from hoping and waiting. More out of routine than inclination, she reached out for her purse to fish out her phone. She fumbled through the pockets but it was nowhere to be found. She tried hard to remember where she had used it last and that's when it struck her that she had placed it on the table in Akriti's office. A wave of panic overtook her. What if Dev had called on her number and someone else had picked it up? She had no way to get in touch with Akriti except for shooting her an email, although she trusted

Akriti to cover up for her in case Dev called. She had to get the phone somehow otherwise she could land up in a lot of trouble. Her thoughts were in overdrive as she quickly changed and grabbed her purse to head out. Bauji would again ask questions but there was no time to worry about that right now. It was almost 5 p.m. and the office would close in a while. She would then have to wait until the next day to get the phone back, and that could be disastrous.

'Bauji, I have to get some vegetables from the market. I'll be back in a while,' she muttered as she rushed out of the house. He watched her go out but said nothing. Luckily for her, the traffic was scarcer than usual and it didn't take her too long to reach Ravenhouse. She had the change ready in her hand as the auto halted outside the building and she made a mad dash up the stairs and down the corridor to Akriti's office, hoping against hope that it wasn't locked already.

'I knew you would come, Renu,' Akriti smiled as Renu almost stumbled past the door in her office, huffing and puffing and panting. The phone was right where she had left it and Renu heaved a sigh of relief, thanking Akriti as she picked up the phone.

'I have to head back right now. I'll call you later, okay?' Renu she said and headed out of the door, her phone tightly in the grip of her palm.

She'd have to rush back as quickly as she'd come and probably pick up some vegetables on the way too, just to keep up with her flimsy alibi. Her pace was frantic and despite the corridor being wide enough, she collided into a body that seemed very familiar. She looked up and saw Arjun's face staring down at her.

'Arjun! What are you doing here?' she blurted out, perplexed.

'Ah, well!' Arjun was unusually calm and his calmness perturbed her even more. *What was he doing here? Had he been following her?* Her instincts told her that something was definitely wrong somewhere.

'Arjun, tell me please. What are you doing here?' she repeated, a little firmly this time.

Arjun held her by the hand and led her down the corridor. 'Where are we going?' she asked frantically, but Arjun just led her on until they entered the lift and reached the topmost floor.

'But this is . . .'

'My office. Ravenhouse Publishers,' he said looking deep into her eyes. 'I own this place, Maya.'

This wasn't something she had seen coming and it left her stunned in silence for a good few minutes. Her heart almost sank to her stomach.

'But, but . . .' Renu's eyes darted wildly around the room, trying to make sense of what was happening. Her head seemed to feel light and heavy at the same time, as Arjun's face swam hazily before her eyes. A frenzy of thoughts passed through her mind, each clashing with the others. As she waited for Arjun to speak, she imagined all kinds of plausible explanations but none of them made complete sense in her head.

Pausing for a few seconds, Arjun looked at her in the eye and said, 'I knew who you were when I came to your house as a tenant. I am no hardware dealer, Renu. I'm just another guy in awe of you.'

Renu's mouth felt like sandpaper as she struggled to find words. *This man knew her secret. He knew everything? What if . . .?*

'Wait, what? *So* you lied to me about who you are?' Her head was reeling now. She leaned back towards the wall behind her for support, unsure of how she should deal with it. Arjun's confession kept playing in her mind while she braced herself for what he would say next.

'I just wanted to know you closely. I swear I wouldn't have if I had known I'd fall in love with you.'

LOVE? Renu couldn't help but feel threatened in his presence now. Here was a man who had lied to her and her family about his identity just so that he could be close to her. What exactly did he want from her? Was he out to harm her? All of a sudden, Renu's guard went up. She had a million things to take care of so that the family name didn't get tarnished. What had she done, she cursed herself. What would happen now?

'Arjun, this is bizarre. Why would you do this? Do you realize how scary this is for me? Tell me the truth, Arjun—what do you really want?'

'I only want you, Maya,' he replied softly.

Renu looked into his large, hypnotic eyes, begging them for help, to make sense of the emotions surging inside her.

'But you . . .' she mumbled.

'I know I didn't tell you the truth when I came to your house the first time but I would never harm you. You know that, Renu. There's something magical between us. You know that too. But if you say that there isn't, I'll fade away just as quickly as I came into your life. You'll never see me again I promise you . . .' he said, as if reading her mind.

'I can't . . . I just can't . . . It's not possible. I can't deal with this Arjun. You lied! I can't deal with this!' Renu said and stormed out of the office. Like always, Arjun had given her too many emotions to process all at once, and she needed to be alone to allow the hurricanes inside her head to settle.

On the way back home, she barely noticed herself being flung from one side to another of the auto rickshaw with every turn. She handed over the fare to the auto driver in a trance and rushed to her room, switching off the lights and locking the door from inside. In those moments of chaos, it was only darkness that offered her the solace she needed. In darkness, she could see what she couldn't see under glaring lights. Darkness stirred her instincts.

She sat at the edge of the bed, closed her eyes and instantly felt calmer. Her thoughts slowed down to a pace where they became clearer, and she could organize them in a coherent sequence. She spoke to herself standing in front of the mirror, like one would speak to a loyal confidant. She realized that there was a part of her that knew almost all the answers to the questions festering inside her.

It was almost dinner time by the time she could feel some semblance of normalcy return. 'Mama, I'm hungry!' Avi whined. He had just walked in after spending an evening in the park with his friends. His face was sweaty and soiled, but Renu allowed him to have dinner before he washed up. After feeding the children, she served dinner in another plate and took it to Bauji's room. Bauji looked at his wristwatch with an annoyed expression on his face. She would normally give him an explanation as to why she was a few minutes late, but today, she did not have any energy to do so. She felt drained beyond measure. She just placed the plate on the table beside his bed along with a glass of water and made her way out without saying a word.

Renu waited rather impatiently for everyone to settle in bed. Once she was sure that all the lights were off, she quietly crept up the stairs to Arjun's room, hoping he'd still be awake. To her surprise, she found him standing on the terrace.

'I knew you would come,' he said softly, before Renu could utter a single word.

'I think I overreacted today. I shouldn't have. I just came to apologize,' she said.

'No, you didn't overreact, Renu. Anyone in your place would have done the same. I am sorry I didn't speak the truth to you but I won't apologize for coming here,' he replied. 'But what anyone else would have missed, you didn't.'

'And what's that, Arjun?' Renu asked.

'The love I have for you. You see it in my eyes, don't you?' Arjun said, locking his gaze with hers.

He leaned closer to her, and Renu flinched a little, not out of discomfort but out of the inexplicable currents coursing through her body with each advancing step of his. She could smell him from where she stood and her mind was torn between fleeing out of the door on the terrace and never coming back, or giving in to the desire that was flooding her senses. That happened every time he was close to her. For better or for worse, Renu realized that her body had decided for itself.

She didn't resist when he grabbed her by the waist almost desperately and pulled her body close to his. So close that she could feel his manhood swelling against her. His raw aroma sent her senses into a tizzy and she raised her heels to lock her lips with his. They devoured each other hungrily. Her chest was heaving and she was breathing heavily. A soft moan of surrender escaped her lips as Arjun's hands slid upwards from her waist and framed the underside of her breasts.

She let go of the tensions in her muscles and threw herself forward, only to be caught by his strong arms. 'I want you, Maya. I want you really bad. I have never wanted anyone more than this, ever.'

'Shh . . . Stop talking, Arjun. Just do what you are doing,' she panted as she pulled herself closer into him, grabbing him by his hair and thrusting her tongue almost violently into his mouth.

She then dragged him to a cement platform at the edge of the terrace without letting go of him and lay on it, pulling his body on top of hers. His hands felt warm and rough gliding over her smooth stomach. She flinched as a wave of arousal engulfed her body but kept her eyes shut, waiting for his hands to caress her full bosom. But he was in no mood for gentle lovemaking. He turned her around on her back and plunged his face into the nape of her neck. Kissing. Biting. The friction from his stubble caused her delicate skin to burn but this was exactly the way she liked it. She grabbed him by his hair and pulled him in closer, taking in his manly scent and feeling the heat of his breath, which smelt of hunger and desperation

Within minutes, her saree, blouse and panties, all lay strewn on the terrace, her petticoat hitched around her waist. Arjun's nails dug deep into the softness of her thighs, and her back arched in raw carnal pleasure. He traced every rivet of her spine with his fingers, and she felt all her knots coming undone. Her body writhed with pleasure under his weight as he entered her without warning, sending her into throes of passion. Her hips involuntarily raised themselves to invite him in and strong waves alternating between frenzy and calm took over her body as he thrust himself into her.

Their bodies moved in perfect rhythm, like the verses of a poem, until she felt hot, liquid salvation course through her veins. Renu threw her head back and let out a loud moan while Arjun pulled her limp body back into his. This was a first for her and she neither had the strength, nor the will to resist it. At that moment, she knew this was what she really wanted. Arjun gave her what Dev never did, and she could no longer silence the call of her body. It didn't matter to her that Arjun had lied to get close to her, in that moment she was just glad that he did. Her body and her soul was starved for love, and in that hunger, few other things made sense. She believed every word he said, and the love he said he had for her.

After that night, Renu would quietly make her way up to the terrace every night and lean against the iron railing to catch the breeze. Arjun would soon sneak up behind her, grab her waist from behind, cup her breasts with his large hands and muffle her urgent moans with forceful bruising kisses. The two would make mad, uninhibited unapologetic love under the stars, with not a care in the world. In that moment, Renu would forget her reality and Arjun would be under her spell—to love her, relish her, and pleasure her every whim until she was breathless and could take no more. They would then lie side-by-side in the silence of the night, savouring the aftertaste of each other's essence and go back to their realities before the crack of dawn. Renu discovered that she hadn't slept so peacefully in years—her body seemed to hover in the air and her mind transcended into a perpetual trance-like state. Arjun had taken over her imagination like a storm. Storms were almost always destructive, she knew, but she could not resist this deluge of sensations crashing against her mind and her body with him in her life. She wanted to be swayed by the wild whirlwinds and surrender to the force of desire that had resurrected within her, like a dormant volcano stirring back to life after ages. Every night, after coming back from her rendezvous with Arjun, she felt that elusive spark flirting with her again. And she would pour herself out on sheets of paper frantically, like the world was ending soon, and she had to put her thoughts on paper before it did. She realized she wasn't writing mechanically any more.

Maya had found her muse.

with Arjun, she felt differently... (faded text from previous page bleeding through)

TEN

In Arjun, Renu had found the love she had been craving for all these years and yet, her heart never felt free of doubt and moments of trepidation. She couldn't quite make out whether what was eating her insides were her own insecurities and self-doubt, or whether her instincts were trying to tell her something.

'What am I to you, Arjun?' Renu asked one day as their bodies lay entwined on Arjun's bed.

'Everything,' he replied, drawing her closer.

'And what does everything mean to you, Arjun?' she asked again.

'Everything means everything. I need you, Renu.'

'What for?'

'For everything.' His voice had a depth and earnestness that always managed to put her constant internal strife to rest, even if for just a little while.

80

Renu picked up a silk cushion and hit Arjun squarely in the face with it as he laughed mischievously. Then she grabbed his hair and pulled his body into hers, clawing his bare shoulders with her nails. 'Don't you ever leave me, okay? Or else I'll kill you and then myself,' she said to him, in a whisper dripping with lust.

'I never will,' he replied as he dug his lips into the nape of her neck, breathing her in. 'Now you tell me. What am I to you?' he hummed, gazing imploringly at her large, kohl-lined eyes. Renu stared back at him, flinching for a moment. She didn't answer that question; at least not then. She wasn't sure she even knew the answer.

That night, like most other nights, Renu lay on the bed, her eyes fixated on the slowly whirring fan on the ceiling and her mind, a conundrum of thoughts. *What is he to me?* She questioned herself. Was he a fantasy? An outlet for her unfulfilled desires? Or, was he more than that? The edge of her lips curled into an involuntary smile as her heart answered that question for her.

That was the moment she realized that she was in love with Arjun—totally, irrationally and irrevocably in love with him. And she knew he was in love with her too; she could so clearly see it in his eyes, hear it in his voice and feel it in his touch. He touched her in a way no one else had. In places she didn't even know existed within her. He touched her without using his hands. He touched her fears, her scars and her vulnerabilities. He touched her soul.

She was taken over by this overwhelming desire to be one with him.

'I wish you could be mine,' Arjun said one evening, as he ran his rough fingers through her magnificent black mane. He had such deep longing in his eyes that all she wanted to do was to fuse her soul with him.

'I am yours, Arjun. I will always be yours,' she said, pulling him closer and burying her face into his chest. What solace she found there! 'But you know we can never be together as man and wife.'

'Yes, I know. You cannot leave your family and your children and I don't want you to do that either. I have you by my side and that's enough for me.'

Renu's eyes turned misty as the reality of their relationship dawned upon her yet again. Were they meant to be like parallel lines—always moving together but destined to never meet? She could now not imagine a life without him. He fulfilled her so. However, given her current situation, it wasn't a possibility. It just wasn't.

'Are we doomed to stay apart like this, Arjun?'

'We are not doomed, Renu. We are blessed to have found each other. We might not belong to each other in a worldly sense, but we will always belong with each other. You are mine, forever,' he smiled as he lifted her chin with his finger and sucked her lower lip into his mouth. Renu moaned gently as she felt every muscle of her body loosen up into sweet surrender. Arjun grabbed the sides of her waist with both hands and pushed her against a wall, crushing her against himself. They gazed into each other's eyes as they kissed, an aura of longing and hunger engulfing them. She could never have enough of him. And that was probably what worried her.

'I feel scared, Arjun,' she said to him one day as they lay on his bed.

'Scared of what? Scared of me?'

'No. Scared of losing you.'

'I will never leave you. Don't let those thoughts even enter your head,' he said calmly.

'You know, I wonder. Is all this we have even real or, is it just an illusion? An escape?'

'You are not my escape, Renu. You are my reality. I love you with my heart and my soul. And that is a fact, more real than reality.'

'You soothe me with your voice and rake up a storm with your words,' she whispered into his ears.

Arjun wrapped his arms around her and ran his fingers through her hair. He held her like that for a long time, until her doubts settled down, like they always did, and she felt reassured again. She needed to be reminded often, and Arjun understood. He was patient. Sometimes Renu wondered how he was so in sync with her that he knew exactly what she wanted to hear at the moment.

She had never been loved like this by a man; so intensely and passionately that she felt like surrendering her entire being to him. His were the arms she wanted to crumble into. His was the voice that tugged at her heartstrings. Every time she looked into his eyes, she saw herself the way she always wanted to see herself—beautiful, precious, desired . . .

She saw herself as Maya.

ELEVEN

'Your daughter is turning out just like you. Just taste this tea she has made! It tastes like urine,' Bauji hissed angrily.

'If you wanted tea, you should have called me, Bauji. Please don't ask Aneisha to do all this. She has exams coming up!' Renu shot back.

'She can top all the exams she wants to but women will always do what women are meant to do,' Bauji replied in a flat voice.

Renu could feel the rage building up inside her. This man had done enough to damage her but she would not, under any circumstances, let him do the same to her daughter.

'Aneisha will not make tea for you or do any other housework,' Renu almost found herself yelling. It wasn't like her to speak to her father-in-law like that. No matter what Bauji said or did, she would always keep her tone polite and respectful. But today, she wasn't about to hold back. She walked out of the hall and into her room before Bauji had a chance to reply. *I have to talk to Dev about this*, she murmured to herself. She wasn't about to let a frustrated old man dictate terms to her daughter.

'Dev, we need to talk,' she spoke abruptly to her husband who had his face buried in a newspaper. He did not look up to respond. It had been several weekends since he had come home, but his presence or absence made little difference to Renu now. He would either go out to meet his friends or lose himself in television shows, one after the other. She could see that he mostly kept to himself, communicating only functionally with Renu and the children; although he would make some time for Bauji in the morning and evening over tea out of a sense of responsibility.

'Dev!' Renu said, a little more loudly this time.

'Sachin Tendulkar scored a century in yesterday's match. I missed it!' Dev was speaking to himself.

'I don't care. I'm trying to talk to you about something important,' she said, her voice agitated. Dev's detachment and indifference was nothing new but it had begun getting to her and she did not know how to deal with it.

'Renu . . . Renu . . . Renu. Why do you keep nagging me all the time? I work hard throughout the week and I get only one day to read the newspaper in peace. And here you come, bothering me with your petty household problems.'

'Is your father a petty household problem?'

'Don't you dare say such things about Bauji!' Dev said, raising his voice. 'He's old and he's our responsibility. And you know that very well.'

'I have never shunned my responsibilities towards him, Dev but he cannot ask Aneisha to fetch him tea when she has board exams coming up. Every minute is precious.'

The anger lines on Dev's face softened a little. 'I'll tell him not to do that. But you have to be polite with him. You have to adjust and be respectful to him. Be mature, Renu.'

Renu kept mum, her heart seething with anger and hurt. Why had it all turned against her? *She was being rude? She was supposed to adjust and compromise? She needed to be mature?* She walked out of the room in a huff and out into the garden without saying a word because she didn't want to start another argument with Dev. And even though he had been cold and distant throughout his stay, she didn't want to make things unpleasant in the little time they had. She stopped her tears from flowing but she felt lonely and alienated in her own house. She needed someone to talk to, someone who'd understand her and hold her hand. She did not have friends she could turn to. Bauji did not appreciate her talking much with other women in the neighbourhood, and sometimes Renu would stand alone on the terrace in the evenings and look on enviously as groups of women chatted and took walks together. She imagined herself as a part of one such group and wondered if that superficial chatter actually helped those women take their minds off the numbing banalities of life, even if for just a little while.

She looked upwards towards the terrace and remembered Arjun. Yes, she had Arjun. But he wouldn't be home at that hour. She pulled out her phone and quickly dialled his number.

'Yes, Renu?' Just hearing him call out her name was enough to soothe her nerves.

'I miss you,' she whispered.

'Okay,' came the reply.

'Okay? Just okay? Don't you miss me too?' she prodded jokingly.

'Of course. I am a little busy. We'll talk later?' he said curtly.

'I love you,' she said, but Arjun had already disconnected the call. *He must be surrounded by people*, she told herself. She would have him back once her husband left. She pulled up a garden chair and immersed herself in thoughts of Arjun, and before she knew it, all the anger and frustration dwindled away into oblivion and her soul was engulfed with peace and joy. Her heartbeat, though a little out of tune in his absence, seemed to calm her down and her eyelids dropped down like heavy curtains as she relived those beautiful moments spent with him. In secret. In a world that was their own. A world where no ugliness existed. There was only love, and beauty, and happiness, and ecstasy. That's the effect Arjun had on her. She didn't know how and when, but he had become the only oasis of hope and happiness in her dreary existence.

She breathed in the crisp autumn air, the familiar smoky scent of it penetrating her nostrils. Autumn in Lucknow had smelt that way every year, ever since she could remember. And every year, it brought along a strange nostalgia. A medley of bitter-sweet memories. It was the same scent that surrounded her when she had gone for long evening walks with her parents, talking, laughing and prancing around them; getting an occasional reprimand for straying too close to the busy road. It was the same scent that surrounded her the day her parents told her that they had decided to part ways. She was all of thirteen and they had decided to send her to a boarding school, right here in Lucknow. She remembered clearly how they had made it seem like a heavenly place to be in, with a bunch of friends, a nice room to herself and the one thing she treasured most—freedom. She had begun to look forward to it already, although she couldn't understand why she couldn't stay with either of them when they were living in the same city. *Hostel is going to be fun*, she told herself, fighting against the doubt, fear and anxiety that were clouding her mind. *But why did she have to go there?*

As days turned into weeks and weeks into months, the answers slowly revealed themselves. Her parents did not want her any more. They now lived separate lives with different partners and there was no place for her in this happy little picture in either of their lives. She was the burden. The odd ball. Someone who could never fit in with their plans. Someone who was not welcome in their lives any more. Youth whizzed past her before she could even make sense of herself. Like a lost, anchorless ship, she sailed wherever the tides took her. She briefly found purpose in her job as a teacher but that too was taken away from her when she married Dev. It wasn't like she regretted marrying Dev, at least not until recently. Dev had given her the stability of things she had always yearned for—a home, a family, a place to call her own where she was wanted and needed.

Dev returned to Sitapur the next day, and Renu's excitement knew no bounds when she heard Arjun's car getting into the driveway that evening. She quickly wiped her face with her dupatta and tucked the stray locks of hair behind her ears before running out to meet the man she loved. They had been apart only for a couple of days, and yet it had seemed like eternity.

'I have missed you so much,' she whispered as her arms coiled around him in a tight embrace once they reached his room.

'I have missed you, too,' he said, gently kissing her forehead. Just the sound of his voice was enough to tranquillize her soul. When she was with him, the sky looked a little bluer than usual and the world, a lot more colourful. The air around them carried the scent of hope—as if all she ever wanted and needed was in the safe confines of his arms.

'What happened? You look tense,' she gently asked Arjun, noticing the stress lines on his face and the slight dullness in his eyes. He looked like he hadn't slept well in a few days.

'Nothing, it's nothing,' he replied a bit too hastily and pried himself out of her embrace.

'I don't believe you. There is something definitely bothering you,' she urged him to speak.

'I said it's nothing. Now will you please stop nagging?' It wasn't like Arjun to talk to her like that. His words pierced her heart but his eyes clearly told her that he was under enormous stress.

For a moment she contemplated leaving him alone to calm down, but how could she? This was the time he probably needed her the most. How could she walk out on him? All she wanted to do was to comfort him and take away all his sorrows. Seeing him like that broke her heart and made her feel helpless.

'Is it something I did, Arjun? Are you angry with me?' she inquired. Arjun had been particularly moody and unpredictable of late, and his changed behaviour baffled her.

'Does everything always have to be about you? What are you so self-absorbed, Renu?' he said in a low voice heavy with sadness. His words hurt her but she was quick to realize her folly. *How could she make this about herself?*

'Sorry. I'm so sorry, Arjun. It's just that I'm very worried for you,' she said, without wasting a moment. Arjun did not reply.

She took a deep breath and sat beside him on the bed, measuring the words in her head so as to not upset him. She no longer knew what would set him off, and she often found herself walking on eggshells around him.

'Arjun, is there anything I can help you with? Please tell me. I'll do anything for you.'

Arjun turned towards her and stared at her face for a few moments. 'Just stay with me, okay? Don't go anywhere. You are my biggest asset,' he said very gently.

And just like that, things went back to being the way they were.

The two locked themselves into each other's arms and lay still for a long, long time. Sometimes she felt she knew Arjun down to his bones but there were times he threw her completely off the hook. He made her question herself, and her own sanity. But he also showered her with so much love that it made everything else vanish into a blur. Little did she know that the hopes and dreams she was building around Arjun were like a beautiful piece of woodwork infested with termites from within—hollow and just waiting to collapse. But there was a learning curve to that too.

TWELVE

Renu caressed Arjun's face with her fingers as she gazed into his eyes. Her lips were aching for a kiss but Arjun turned his face away. It had been a few days since their last meeting and the respite that she'd had was brief. Arjun had gone back to being rude and distant, and his treatment of her oscillated between intense love and cold indifference. He still looked harrowed, and wouldn't speak a word about it. It was a weekday and he was at home. She had noticed that he had also become infrequent at work. Renu's anxiousness was growing by the day as she tried to coax him into sharing his woes.

'I'm going to lose everything. Everything!' he said abruptly.

'What? Why?' Renu almost yelled, although she was glad that Arjun was finally opening up to her.

'Nothing can be done. There is no way out,' he continued, as if talking to himself, pacing up and down the room.

'Will you at least tell me what happened?' she asked in a voice tinged with anxiety and concern for him.

'Nothing,' he said and pulled away. Renu grabbed him by the shoulders and turned him around to face her. She cupped his face gently with her hands and asked him again, piercing his eyes with her gaze.

'Why do you want to know?' he asked.

'I don't know. I may be able to help you. If nothing else, I can be a support to you.'

'Okay, so my publishing house is running into huge losses and I am going bankrupt. I am going to lose everything. Now what? Is there anything you can do about it?' He was impatient and fidgety, she noticed. And his tone was accusatory, as if Renu was the reason for his problems.

'Calm down, Arjun. Only then will you find a way.'

'There is no way, Renu. I am in serious debt. And the only way I can repay it is by selling the publishing house!'

'Wait a minute. Don't take any decision in haste. You've built this up from scratch; it is something you've always wanted.'

'It doesn't matter any more . . .'

'Okay, why don't you take up a part-time job or something alongside? Maybe that'll ease the burden till you find a more permanent solution?' she offered meekly. She knew that whatever she was suggesting was meaningless, but what else could she do in that moment?

'I don't want a job! I don't want to work for someone else. I have enough on my hands. Please leave me alone for some time.'

Renu stepped away hesitantly. *What had happened to Arjun? Her Arjun.* She had never seen him so distraught and so out of sorts. It was like the world around him was crumbling, while she looked on helplessly. She felt powerless to do anything to stop it. She made her way downstairs, feeling heavy and restless in the heart. The kids were about to reach home and it was time for lunch. She absent-mindedly laid out the utensils on the table and went into the kitchen to cut some salad. But all this while, her thoughts were with Arjun. What had happened to make him behave so?

After lunch, when she had tucked the children in for their afternoon nap, she spent hours mulling over his words. There had been a definite change in his behaviour. He was not the same Arjun she had come to love. Had the crisis stressed him out so much? Was there nothing she could do to help him? Of course, she could. She had some savings.

Have you lost it, Renu? What if Dev finds out? A voice spoke from within her but she wasn't going to pay it any heed. She loved Arjun with her body, heart and soul. Everything that was hers was his. She was his. What was money for anyway? Money could always be earned again but she knew that if Arjun's business sank, he would be devastated and that thought terrified her to no end. Her concern for Arjun was bigger than her fear of ruining her marriage; it was bigger than anything she had ever known.

All she ever wanted was to see Arjun happy and smiling again. Those stress lines on his face twisted her heart in myriad ways; she just couldn't bear to see him in that state.

THIRTEEN

'Hey, Renu!' It was Akriti on the other end of the phone. It had been a few weeks since Renu had visited her in the office, but it always felt good hearing Akriti's warm voice.

'Yes, Akriti. Tell me,' Renu replied. Akriti was a bright, boisterous soul and her enthusiasm was quite contagious. Talking to her, Renu felt happy, happier than she had felt anytime lately. For a second, she contemplated asking Akriti about the company finances, but then quickly backtracked. She wasn't sure if Arjun wanted his employees to be privy to it. In her impatience and desperation, she didn't want to do anything that would make the situation worse for him.

Arjun's blow-hot-blow cold vibes had been constantly gnawing at her heartstrings, eating her up inside. She couldn't figure out where she had gone wrong and why the perfect bond they had shared was slipping away while she looked on helplessly. There were days when Arjun would drown her in enough love and passion to erase all sense of logic and good sense from her head and then in a heartbeat, he would turn into a stranger—cold, distant, indifferent and aloof—treating her as if she did not even exist.

'Okay, there's this Lit Fest coming up in the city three months from now and I wanted to ask if you'd like to make an appearance there,' Akriti asked enthusiastically, bringing her back from her meandering thoughts.

'An appearance? But that would mean . . .' Renu's heart filled with a mortifying dread at the mere thought. What was Akriti getting at? She couldn't possibly!

'Yes, we think it would be a good opportunity for Maya to come out with her real identity, if you want to, that is. It would generate a lot of buzz, which of course, is good for both you and us.'

'Akriti, we've talked about this before. You know my situation all too well . . .' Renu's voice trailed off. The mere thought of her family finding out about her alternate identity made her break into a cold sweat. Nobody in the family would accept it, and how would she ever face Dev? What would her children think? And Bauji, she could not even imagine how he would react. He'd probably die of shame. The last thought seemed more like a silver lining and Renu quickly dismissed it from her mind before it grew large enough to become an incentive for her to actually go ahead and take up the offer.

'There's no compulsion and no hurry, Renu. Take your time to think about it. It's perfectly fine if you don't want to do it, we'll still respect your decision, as always.

But remember, if you do this, it would mean larger book advances, more sales and all the perks that come with being a celebrity author,' said Akriti before she hung up the phone.

Larger book advances. Bigger royalty cheques. Celebrity author. It was all too tempting but the stakes were too high. It wasn't like she needed a lot of money. Dev sent her enough money to run the household, albeit on a tight budget, and she could always dive into her earnings for the occasional indulgence. She had very few personal needs. She did not splurge on mindless shopping or expensive spa treatments. But she did like to buy nice clothes for Aneisha and toys for Avi. She wanted to give her children all those things she never got as a child. Whatever she earned from her books, lay safely stashed in her secret bank account. That money would come in handy when it was time for the children to go to college. She hadn't decided what explanation she'd offer to Dev, and hoped to come up with a plausible story by the time they got to that point. Bauji, hopefully, would have left for his heavenly abode by then.

Renu was appalled at the darkness of her own thoughts regarding Bauji. It wasn't like she wished ill upon him but the old man was like a perpetual thorn in her ankle; a shackle that fettered her freedom and a major obstacle to a peaceful existence for everyone around him.

But more than anything else, more money would mean she could help Arjun with his financial problems.

~

It had been three days since Arjun had come home. He hadn't even bothered to inform her where he was going and when he'd be back. Earlier, he would always meet her before he went anywhere and call her frequently, often every few hours. But nowadays he just came and went off at will, leaving her pining and often worried for him. *He must be under tremendous stress*, she would tell herself but her own explanations did not sound convincing even to her. A part of her brain always kept telling her that she was living in a fool's paradise. Nevertheless, she missed his presence so much that she would often go up to his room all alone, just to breathe in his scent. She would sit there for hours, sometimes cleaning up his room, folding his clothes and lying on his bed, imagining him lying next to her, stroking her hair while she curled her limbs around his.

'Maa, what are you doing here?' Aneisha's voice startled Renu and she quickly sprang up from Arjun's bed and began straightening her clothes. The guilt on her face was comparable to what it would have been if Arjun had actually been lying right next to her.

'N . . . n . . . nothing. The room was lying unlocked and there was water dripping somewhere so I just came upstairs to check. Nobody's here,' she added instinctively, her mind crowded with guilt and she wondered if her body language betrayed her words.

'Okay . . .' replied Aneisha, a confused expression about her face. 'I wanted to give you this list of things that I need for the science project. I have to submit it by tomorrow.'

Renu took the piece of paper from her daughter's hands and unfolded it to read the contents. 'Okay. I'll go to the market right now,' she smiled. A trip to the market would perhaps be just the distraction she needed to get Arjun out of her mind, at least temporarily.

It was early evening when Renu got herself an auto from the crossing a short walk away from her house. Just as the auto rickshaw was about to move, she saw something off the corner of her eye that made her heart skip a beat.

'Stop! Stop!' she yelled at the auto wallah.

'But, madam, I haven't even started yet,' he retorted, rather bemused.

Renu peered out of the auto rickshaw and navigated her gaze through the maze of evening traffic. There, on the other side of the road, stood Arjun, locked in an embrace with a young beautiful woman who appeared to be in her twenties. Renu got off the auto and stood frozen across the street, battling with her mind to make sure that what she was witnessing was just a horrible nightmare, and not a twist of destiny.

Arjun planted a kiss on the woman's cheek before he started to cross the road, at which point his gaze met Renu's. He flinched for a moment and then nonchalantly made his way towards the house. Renu deliberated between following him home and confronting him, or going to the market to fetch the list of things her daughter had given her. She knew going to the market was urgent, and yet the searing fire in her heart made her retrace her steps back home and right up to Arjun's room.

FOURTEEN

'Who was that woman, Arjun? And where were you all these days?' Renu demanded, a little surprised at the tone of her own voice since she had never spoken like that even to Dev. But with Arjun, she felt a strange sense of ownership, like he was hers and hers alone and could belong to nobody else. Just as she was his. Upon seeing him with another woman, her possessiveness had taken on a new form. Jealousy consumed her, and she found herself quickly losing control of her thoughts.

'And how exactly is that any of your concern?' replied Arjun coldly. His unpredictable demeanour always threw her off course.

'How does that concern me? Of course, it concerns me, Arjun! I thought you said you loved me, and now you, you are cheating on me with that young girl!' Renu screamed, her eyes welling up with hot tears.

'Renu . . . Renu . . . Renu,' Arjun's voice was uncomfortably calm, 'you are a married woman. You know there is no future for us in the real world. I do love you but I have to settle down with someone for real, right?'

'How could you do this to me, Arjun? You know what this makes you? A liar and a cheat!'

'Says the woman who is having an extramarital affair with her tenant,' said Arjun icily, his words piercing her heart like a thousand needles.

Renu stared at him aghast, unable to believe her ears.

But what Arjun had said was actually the naked, heartbreaking truth and there was no getting away from it. She knew. Who was she to demand fidelity when she was herself the infidel? And what exactly was she really expecting out of this relationship? She couldn't divorce Dev and did she expect Arjun to wait on her forever?

Reality suddenly hit her like a bolt in the chest. She felt claustrophobic and short of breath. Arjun wasn't wrong but what about their love, what about the moments they had shared, the promises he had made? She had been so lost drifting in the tides of his love that the thoughts of the future hadn't even crossed her mind. Arjun had proclaimed his intense love for her, as had she, but where were they going with this? There were no concrete plans, no vision, no goals . . . Her head reeled and cold beads of sweat appeared on her forehead.

She knew they would probably never get to spend a life together, but she was also sure that there would never come a time when she would stop loving him. Regardless of the harsh reality and social conventions, she had dreamt of having Arjun by her side, always. She thought she didn't have expectations from him, until he stabbed her with his actions and then his words. The words hurt more.

It took just one crack for her castle of illusions to come crashing down like a house of cards, each splinter piercing her soul over and over again. The dreamy clouds had lifted, giving way to blinding clarity that was so bright that it was unbearable. That's the thing about truth—it doesn't flinch, it doesn't falter, it sears and burns. And the truth singed her heart, scarring it in places she never even realized existed.

It finally dawned upon her that Arjun had used her. He had taken advantage of her vulnerability and used her loneliness as a crutch to feed his own monsters. He had sucked the lifeblood out of her soul with his lies and manipulations. It was all too clear, blinding even—just like the love she had for him.

She had given him all that she had; her mind, her body, her soul and everything else in between until she had nothing left in her she could call her own. And yet, he had so conveniently dumped her for another woman. Despite all she had given him, he did not want to be hers.

'But you still love me, right?' she croaked between tears. She could not believe she was still asking him this but her mind, her heart and her words seemed to have all dissociated from each other.

'Yes, I love you,' said Arjun wrapping his arms around her, filling her with a sense of calm that she, deep in her heart, knew was as fleeting as a dream. She had loved him more than anything and the mere thought of him going away was unbearable for her. She could not afford to lose him, even if it meant losing herself.

Renu was trying hard to come to terms with the fact that her relationship with Arjun was never exclusive and would not be so in the future. There were and always will be other women, and although she had accepted it as a part of his lifestyle, the very thought consumed her from within. *I have to learn to accept this*, she told herself repeatedly. They still met but it wasn't the same. Renu no longer could be her carefree self around him. Every time she looked into his eyes, her anxieties grew. The gaze that had once comforted her now fed her deepest fears, and over time, she found herself spiralling down a dark vortex.

'Arjun, what am I to you?' she asked him when they were sitting out on the terrace one evening. It wasn't the first time she was asking him this. She had asked him this often and his replies gave her momentary solace, even though her heart knew all too well the brutal truth behind his replies.

'You are my woman, Renu. I will always be with you. You know how you and I transcend every kind of conventional relationship,' he said, predictably.

'And the other women?' Renu felt a little hesitant questioning him because there was no way to guess how he would react. After that day, she had never brought up the subject, and neither had he. But she couldn't brush it under the carpet forever, now that Arjun had become brazen about it.

He would text women in her presence and she would often see him get off cars with different women in the driver's seat each time. It hurt her deeply each time she witnessed it but she could never gather enough courage to confront him, for the fear of him walking away from her for good. She hadn't planned on broaching the issue today—it had just slipped off her tongue, maybe because Arjun was in a pleasant mood.

'You know me by now, Renu. This is me. This is who I am. I am not lying to you or hiding anything. Am I? If I didn't love you, would I ever be this honest with you? Tell me, why would I still be here if I did not love you?' His voice was soft and considerate. 'You know what we have is deep and beautiful. Why lose it over something that doesn't mean anything? I have accepted you for who you are and your reality. Can you not do the same for me?'

The way he spoke, his words cast a spell on Renu. Of course, he was being honest. And the most important thing was that they were together. That's all she wanted and that's all he wanted. Wasn't that perfect?

'But . . . but Arjun . . . you know . . . my feelings for you. It hurts me to see you . . .' Renu trailed off. She wasn't sure if she should have said it at all. Maybe she was pushing her luck too far.

'Renu . . . Renu . . . Renu . . . My Renu,' Arjun smiled warmly. 'Why are you being oversensitive? You know I don't like this kind of over-possessiveness. It turns me off. Is love about possessing someone? Is it about owning someone? Love is free, unfettered, like the air and water. Like our love is,' he said, cupping her face in his hands.

Renu felt her heart weep but she did not allow the tears to find their way into her eyes. She forced a smile and tugged Arjun by the collar of his shirt to pull him closer to her.

Maybe she *was* being oversensitive. Maybe she *was* overreacting. Was she losing her mind? She loved Arjun and he was with her. What more could she possibly want? Why was she being so demanding and irrational? Was love about possession and bondage? Maybe she wasn't evolved enough to love freely like Arjun could. Was her love bordering on obsession?

'I love the way you write, Renu. You know that, don't you?' Arjun said, pulling Renu close to him. She smiled and nodded, immediately distracted from the dark thoughts swirling inside her head.

These were the moments she lived for—when Arjun wasn't being distant and elusive, when she could lose herself and everything about her in him. When he was present with her in mind, body and spirit, showering his love upon her. She knew his love was like a snowflake—a beautiful and meticulously crafted thing that would melt away and disappear the moment it touched the palm of her hand. Every time Arjun pulled away from her abruptly after a brief spell of closeness, he ripped away a part of her soul, and yet, every time he wanted to come close, she let him. Every moment of the long spells of his absence felt like a blunt knife scraping her soul mercilessly and she realized that the excruciating agony was the price she had to pay for the brief moments of togetherness she was ever going to have with him. And she could not stop herself from paying that price.

'So, working on something new lately? You never even tell me about your work. I'm your publisher for heaven's sake!' he joked.

Indeed, she never discussed her work with him. He probably never even got to read her books till they were out in print. It made her happy that Arjun was taking an interest in her work. There were times she just wanted to discuss her writings with someone but apart from Akriti, she had no one.

'Yes, it's almost complete, my new book. All thanks to you,' she said, her cheeks colouring a little.

'Thanks to me? What did I do?'

'Let's say you are my muse, Arjun,' she whispered softly.

Arjun burst out laughing.

'Renu, oh, Renu! I didn't know you loved me so much!' he exclaimed and gathered her into his arms. 'Are you not going to tell me what it's called?'

'It's called "Maya"' she replied.

'Hmm. Interesting. Are you finally writing your autobiography?'

'Well, you'll know when you read it,' Renu said and planted a soft kiss on Arjun's lips. He looked into her eyes and smiled back.

'Are you not going to let me read it?'

'Not now. Later.'

In an instant, Arjun brushed away her arms from around his neck and turned the other way. Renu's heart began to pound. They were having a beautiful moment together and she had ruined it all by making him angry.

She grabbed his arm and turned him around again, cupping his face between her palms and kissing his forehead. 'I'll send it to you today. Please don't be angry,' she said, as if pacifying a child, and within seconds Arjun was smiling again. Although she was terrified of his anger and spontaneous detachment, she found his childlike fussing endearing sometimes. It made her want to love him more, pamper him and protect him. And even when she wanted to, she could never say 'no' to him. He always had his way with her.

~

'Renu! What have you done to yourself?' Akriti remarked when Renu visited her office to discuss some ideas. A couple of months had passed since the first time she had spotted Arjun with another woman.

'What do you mean?' Renu replied in a low voice. Akriti curtly pointed to a mirror at the far end of her office. It had been a while since Renu had noticed her appearance, and the person she saw in the mirror was unrecognizable even to herself. Her long, lustrous hair was in complete disarray like it hadn't seen a hairbrush for days, there were bags as dark and heavy as lead blocks under her eyes and her skin had turned a sickly pale shade of grey with patches all over. Her cotton kurta hung loosely off her shoulders, with the neckline drooping askew since it hardly had any flesh for support.

'Is everything all right?' Akriti asked, her voice heavy with concern. She had known Renu for a long time and the two had grown to be more than just acquaintances. Renu stared back at Akriti in silence, her throat choked with her failing words. Her heart craved for a shoulder to cry on, a patient ear that would listen without judgement and a calm voice that would tell her that she was not alone in her anguish and that everything would be all right soon.

'Is there anything you want to talk about, Renu?' asked Akriti gently, as if reading her mind.

'Maybe. But I don't know where to begin or even how,' Renu trailed off, her eyes darting from one corner of the room to another, just like her thoughts.

'Let's go out somewhere. This office of mine is not really a chatty kind of place, I know. Do you want to grab some coffee? I am hungry,' offered Akriti cheerfully and Renu felt her lips curl up into a slight, hesitant smile. Maybe pouring out her woes to someone would lighten her burdened heart.

'I don't know where to begin, Akriti. Or whether I should even be talking about this at all.' Renu repeated to herself, swirling the stirrer into her coffee rather absent-mindedly, making random patterns in the froth once they were settled at the coffee shop.

'Is it a man problem?' Akriti asked calmly and Renu looked up at her in surprise. With her short perky hair and childlike face, Akriti didn't quite look like an Agony Aunt and yet, there was so much warmth and genuine concern in her eyes that it was difficult to not trust her.

'How did you know?' asked Renu, rather taken aback at her bluntness.

'My dear woman, men are the leading cause of problems in women's lives,' laughed Akriti. 'Tell me . . .'

'It's very complicated . . .'

'Sometimes the most complicated things stem from something very simple. And know one thing, Renu, you are not alone. It happens to most of us at some point. The fancy word for it is *mid-life crisis*.' Renu couldn't help but smile at Akriti's humour. The woman was such a bundle of positive vibes, a ray of sunshine that seemed a welcome change from Renu's own darkened soul.

'You will not judge me, will you?' Renu bit her lips apprehensively.

'Try me,' said Akriti and placed her palm over Renu's hand.

'I am in love with someone who is not my husband . . .'

Akriti listened intently as Renu looked down and poured out every bit of her anguish into her patient ears.

'You are not the only one to go through this, Renu. It happens to many of us. Blame it on middle age; we crave attention, passion and a little bit of adventure, just to escape the mundane flow of life. It's all right!'

Akriti was being pragmatic about the whole thing and Renu was beginning to see her point, somewhat. She was right, Renu couldn't resist the attention Arjun showered upon her when they first met. Her dreary life was devoid of love, and Arjun, with his sweet words and seductive eyes, made her feel desirable like she hadn't felt in a long, long time. There was nothing unusual about that, except . . .

'But why the hell did you have to get emotionally entangled with him?' Akriti asked, even though she was aware of the invalidity of her own question. She knew that nobody gets emotionally entangled out of choice, feelings just happen. They take over you when you least expect them to and by the time you've realized that you are trapped in their clutches, it is too late and too difficult to break free. What had started out as a clandestine affair between Renu and Arjun had grown into something Renu had not even imagined in her wildest dreams.

Then just as Renu was talking, she mistakenly mentioned a name.

'Did you say Arjun?' Akriti cut her short in the middle of a sentence and fished out a photograph from her phone. Renu's description of the man matched someone she knew. 'I hope it is not this man?' It was a group photograph of all the company employees from one of their events. Arjun looked confident and happy, and somehow very different from the Arjun she knew.

Renu nodded her head slightly.

'So by Arjun you meant Arjun Singh Chauhan? The owner of Ravenhouse Publishers? Did I get that right?'

Renu nodded again.

'Are you fucking kidding me!' Akriti let out an exasperated sigh and threw her hands up in the air.

'I wish I was. I really wish I was.'

'Renu, we all know of his delinquent ways. He's seen with a new woman practically every week! But that would still be acceptable if he wasn't such a selfish, emotionally manipulative scumbag. The guy is using you, Renu!' said Akriti with a finality in her voice.

'I know he is using me, Akriti. I know it very well. But how does one use something that belongs to him?'

'Are you crazy, Renu? Don't destroy yourself over this man. You have a family. You have children. Hell, look how beautiful and talented you are. Do you really need to do this to yourself?' Akriti's voice was now impatient, bordering on angry.

'The problem is, I can't stop. Not now. Not any more. My feelings for him . . .' Renu trailed off. Between the two of them, Akriti was the pragmatic one, or so it seemed, while Renu found it hard to stay afloat every time emotions surged up inside her.

'Okay, I may not be as deep and intense as you but let me tell you something—there's a kind of love that makes you go down on one knee, and there's the kind that brings you down on both. You don't need the latter, because no matter what you do, you cannot make anyone love you back.' Akriti's voice was now pensive. Her words made complete sense to Renu. She wasn't telling her something she didn't know already but her helplessness made her angry at herself.

'It feels like a tug of war all the time, Akriti,' said Renu ruefully.

'Then drop your end of the rope.'

'What?'

'Yes, you heard me right; drop your end of the rope! What are you fighting for? The thing you are clinging on to does not even exist and you know it all too well!'

As pathetic as it sounded, Renu knew Akriti was right. What she was clinging on to did not even exist. She realized that she had already become an empty shell of a person with zero self-esteem. She needed to let go or this relationship would destroy her. She needed to drop her end of the rope.

That meeting with Akriti gave her strength and a newfound resolve. Akriti's words only reinforced what she had known all along, and she knew she had just been throttling that little voice of reason. Hearing Akriti say it out aloud made her realize what a fool she had been to not listen to her own instincts. She would end it with Arjun and tell him straight to the face that she wasn't going to pander to him any more. He couldn't use her for his whims and he couldn't romp around town with a number of women and then come to her occasionally like she was some kind of a standby whore. As soon as she reached home, Renu marched straight up to Arjun's room to give him a piece of her spine, only to find him sitting on the bed, his head hung low and tears streaming down his face.

FIFTEEN

In an instant Renu forgot what she had come for, as her love for Arjun clouded her senses. She rushed to gather him in her arms, comfort him, caress him and ask him what had happened.

'My father is no more,' he whispered hoarsely between stifled sobs. It was unusual for Arjun to display so much distress. He was brought up in a conventional Thakur family, where it was considered shameful for boys to cry or display any emotion overtly, except for anger. For Renu, however, it was gut-wrenching to watch her Arjun shattering to pieces. How could she deliver another blow upon him when he already seemed so broken? No, she would never leave his side. She would stand by him no matter what, even if it meant breaking herself to keep him whole.

She drew herself close to him, standing in front of him while he continued sitting on the bed. She took his head comfortingly in her hands, held it against her stomach and ran her fingers through his hair, trying to calm him down. He buried his face in an embrace and it made her shiver slightly. His touch always did that to her.

'Take off your clothes,' he said, still sobbing.

His words threw Renu off for a moment. 'But Arjun . . .'

'Take them off, please. For me,' he pleaded this time, his voice so dense with emotion that Renu did not know how to react. The best she could do at that moment was to oblige him, but something within her didn't feel right. For reasons she couldn't quite fathom yet, it felt degrading and humiliating. The little nagging voice inside her head was screaming in protest but confused and unable to control herself, she slowly began taking off her clothes. Arjun sat there looking at her, his face expressionless. She took some time to undress, trying to read his eyes, but it was devoid of any emotion. He had stopped crying by now and was staring at her naked body intensely, almost like a wild predator.

He ordered her to get on the edge of the bed on all fours, and made her spread her knees wide, before unzipping his pants and penetrating her roughly from behind, without touching her at all with his hands. He just stood there between her legs and pounded her roughly, grunting like an angry animal. It hurt her. Her numbness and shock had made her absolutely dry between her legs. And yet he seemed oblivious to her pain and discomfort. She closed her eyes and swallowed the humiliation, her gut twisting in discomfort and pain. She wanted him to stop but she couldn't tell him, and neither did she understand why he was doing this to her. *Maybe he's not in the right frame of mind*, she consoled herself. After all, he was grieving and not everyone coped with grief the same way. Maybe this would make him feel better? Could she not do this much for the man she loved? She tried to distract herself with all kinds of thoughts while Arjun pounded her like she was an inanimate object. He then grabbed the sides of her waist roughly and dug his nails violently in her skin as he stroked faster and faster and exploded inside her.

When he was done, he pulled himself out and zipped up his pants, without uttering a single word. Renu turned around to look at him, hoping he'd say something now or at least look at her but he seemed to have already zoned out. 'I'll see you later,' he mumbled and walked out of the door abruptly.

Renu limped over in pain to gather her clothes; every fibre of her body felt soaked in shame and humiliation. Arjun had come as a blessing in her life, but at this time, she felt exploited and violated like she had never felt before. She tried hard to justify what had just happened but the toxic cocktail of feelings spiralling inside of her didn't seem to allow for it.

She realized that she had been treated like dirt, when all that she ever had for him was love and longing. In her mind, she had made an excuse for his behaviour even though her mind kept shrieking in defiance. Renu was in a trance where logic had no place. Her heart and her mind were at war with each other and part of her had begun hating herself already for how she still felt for Arjun.

In that moment, Renu realized that her love for Arjun was no longer just that—it had begun bordering on obsession. Urdu poets often talked of the seven stages of love—*hab* (attraction), *uns* (infatuation), *ishq* (love), *aqueedat* (reverence), *ibadat* (worship), *junoon* (obsession), *maut* (death). She remembered another Urdu word—*fanaa*—the destruction of self in love. For a brief moment of sanity, she realized where she was headed. She was headed to her end. For Arjun, she had annihilated her entire being—her dignity, her self-respect, her sense of self, even her identity. And what had she got in return?

She went down to her room, dazed and confused and numb. She felt dirty. Dirtier than she had ever felt in her entire life. She felt this urgent need to cleanse herself of the disgusting filth that she felt shrouding her entire body. She locked herself inside the bathroom, turned the cold shower on, and stepped under it, fully clothed. And stood there like that for a long time, feeling absolutely nothing.

That evening, Renu sat on her bed staring blankly at the wall with eyes that looked dead. Those enormous, doe-eyes had lost their sparkle, that glint of hope that used to often shine through even in the darkest of moments. Her soul was now a lustreless black abyss. Faith had died inside her.

SIXTEEN

'Renuuuuu!' Akriti shrieked over the phone. '*Unbridled Passions* has received a phenomenal response. Most copies got sold out within the first week! You have to do that interview, man!'

Renu could barely manage a smile. She felt empty inside and all the literary success did not seem to matter any more. Her passion seemed to have dried up and she wasn't even sure if she could ever write anything any more. 'Hmm . . . that's great,' she mumbled, her solemnity drowning out Akriti's enthusiasm.

'That's it? That's all you have to say?' Akriti sounded disappointed.

For a few seconds, Renu played with the idea of confiding in Akriti but then decided against it. 'I am excited, Akriti. Very excited. Just a little unwell. Can I call you later?'

'Oh all right. Yeah sure. You take care, woman. I'll talk to you later.'

Renu almost flung her phone onto the bed and made her way to the terrace, desperately feeling in need of some fresh air. She stood by the railing overlooking the park and the sight of children playing cricket distracted her temporarily from her inner turmoil, even if for a moment. Such innocence, she thought to herself, wondering how long before they would lose it forever.

'You really should do that interview, Maya.' It was Arjun's voice closing in on her from behind. Renu drew a deep breath and turned around to face him.

'Don't call me Maya. I am not Maya. I am Renu. Maya is just an illusion, and you know that very well.'

'From where I stand, Renu is an illusion.'

'But that's not who I am! I am Renu, and it would be better if you kept that in mind.'

'Okay, okay, Renu. I think you should do that interview. It will be good for you,' Renu could see the earnestness in Arjun's eyes, and there was nothing that her heart wanted more, or had always wanted. But, what about Bauji? What about Dev? Dev would still understand or come to terms with it in time, but Bauji would never forgive her for soiling the family's reputation.

Renu let out a long exasperated sigh, hoping to diffuse some of the stress along with the air expelled from her lungs.

'You are a talented writer, Renu. It will be very unfair if the world doesn't come to know you.'

'No. I can't do it. I just can't. It's not possible.'

'Fine. Suit yourself. I thought I could depend on you to help me.' Arjun's voice was suddenly cold and he just turned and walked away. Renu was used to his fluctuations by now, even though they tore her apart every time she faced it. But it was just how he was. Coursing through her veins one moment and completely vanishing the next. The cycle exhausted her but she thought she still had the strength to go on, as rocky or as steep as the climb may be.

Renu rushed after him into his room.

'Help you? How?' she turned him around and looked at him with questioning eyes.

'If you make a public appearance and let your identity be known, it will create a huge buzz around the book and spike sales drastically. It could save the publishing house from sinking!'

Renu was rendered speechless for a moment. If there was one thing she could do to help Arjun, it was this. And yet, she felt so tied down and helpless—a little pained too because in her heart she knew what this was about. Arjun didn't really care about her success as an author. All he cared about was saving his business from drowning, even if it meant destroying her life.

'I'll do it,' she said without the slightest bit of trepidation, a little surprised at the resolve in her own words. There was nothing she wouldn't do for Arjun. She could handle Dev, he would understand. And Bauji could just go bite dust.

'Are you sure, Maya?' Arjun's voice was warm again and his eyes softened as he brushed his fingers along her cheeks, under her hair and clasped them together at the back of her neck.

'Renu . . .' she whispered, intoxicated by the heat of his touch. It was like she had one foot chained to her reality and the other one floating amidst the clouds.

'Tell me, will you do it for me?'

'Yes, I will.'

It was Arjun, only Arjun who could starve all her existing fears and give rise to new ones. It had finally dawned upon her that Arjun only wanted her around so that she could use her fame to resurrect his business. And having known him, she wasn't even sure whether there was a crisis at all. He could very well be lying. But, in her love for him, she would do anything that he wanted her to.

SEVENTEEN

Truth and lies are like oil and water. You can shake them up all you want, but they will never mix. At least not for long. Arjun's words never matched his actions, which in turn, never matched his thoughts. In trying to decipher him, Renu found herself trapped in a whirlpool of confusion, and heartbreak that seemed endless. It exhausted her entire being, and sucked out her life, but so consumed was she with Arjun that the idea of seeking a shore did not even cross her mind. She had a lot to say to him, but between them, there was no room for her words. At the same time, she had this intense need to pour herself out. She pulled out a pen and a few sheets of paper—her loyal tools—and began writing. She would, of course, never share this with Arjun.

For my Arjun,

I am sorry for all the times I have said things that hurt you. In hurting you I always end up hurting myself more, but there are times when something inside me gets the better of me. That doesn't mean that I am doubting you, blaming you or trying to accuse you of something—it is just my own foible as a human being manifesting itself. Nothing more, nothing less. Whatever I say or do, I cannot change the fact that I am yours in every conceivable way, whether you keep me in or out, far or near, with or without you.

You are not responsible for my predicament in any way. It is entirely self-inflicted, although I cannot stop wishing that I had some way of dragging myself out of it. You have been honest. You have never made any false promises. You have always kept my expectations in their place. Kept me in my place. And you have been perfect. I wouldn't for the life of me hold you up for this, so please don't feel pressured in any way by my words.

I still don't know what I am to you, and now I won't even ask. Partly because I know you will not answer and partly because I am scared that you just might.

I just want to tell you what's inside of me today, because it is all for you.

In my defence, this is not what I set out for. I thought I had it all covered. I don't know when you started mattering more to me that anything else ever. I don't know when I started caring for you to the extent that I would put everything at stake just to see that smile of yours, even if the cost of that smile were my tears. I don't know why I keep finding my way back to you, even when my mind is screaming in protest.

I just know that I see myself in you. I just know that I want to dissolve in you, like a river into the ocean. It will probably not make much of a difference to you but for me, there is no other abode. No other destiny. That place I keep talking about—that place, far, far away where I belong and where I'll find peace—that place is you, Arjun.

The problem is that out of billions of people in this world, my soul had to choose yours, and that is one fact that cannot be undone, at least not by me. I'm not heartbroken, no—a heartbreak would have felt like a bed of roses compared to this. Heartbreaks can be healed. Lovers can be replaced. Relationships bloom and die, like flowers. But how can I pull myself away from you when my soul is still tied to yours, Arjun, even if yours is not tied to mine. Can you see that you are the luckier one here? Such a travesty, isn't it?

But a fighter that I am, I've tried my best. I've tried everything you can think of and can't, to keep myself in control. To be sane. But sanity and I have never really gotten along, and it is too late in the day to make friends with it now.

You are a difficult person, but it is so surprisingly easy to love you. I may feel enraged at times, and pile on my own hurt and insecurities onto you, but I wouldn't trade you for anything else in the world. In you I see only beauty and I wouldn't have you any other way. To me, you are perfect just the way you are, with your cracks, scars, burn marks and lost pieces. Perfect in your imperfection.

You'll probably call me childish, oversensitive and reckless for this—maybe I am all of that but my emotions are not a slave to my reality. It's my soul that is a slave to my emotions, and I also know that it's not a good thing. Either I feel it, or I don't. Either it is *real, or it isn't. You are lucky to have evolved. I'm, unfortunately, way behind you on this.*

But I must admit that sometimes it gets weary. I sometimes get tired of hiding my pain behind fake smiles, and crying myself to sleep once the noise inside my head subsides a little. Putting up a brave face in front of you, and pretending to be fully in control of myself. Not talking about how I feel because I just can't, because I am not allowed to. Not being able to talk myself out of it because it isn't a simple matter of heart or mind, or mind over matter—you are a journey my soul is determined to take, for better or for worse. You are my destiny—my beginning and also my end.

But I'll tell you what you are not—you are not the cause of my pain. It is my own expectations—an undesirable side effect of loving someone. I was hoping to go at it alone but this wretched existence wouldn't let me. Mine is a very ordinary kind of love really, which is because I am an ordinary person—a little extra ordinary maybe, not extraordinary. Ordinarily insane love; the kind that comes with hurt and hope in equal measures.

I know you have your battles to fight and I have mine. But in your pain and agony, I forget my own. The thing about scars is that you cannot make them go away—you can only learn to live with them. And it is easier sometimes when you have a hand to hold, that's all. I have never asked you to share what you don't want to, and I never will. I just want to do whatever I can in my capacity to make it better for you—that's the only real urge I have left.

I know that this is not easy for you, and also that I have a little place in your heart, even if it's buried in a small dark dusty corner. You may not say it or show it, but it seeps out sometimes, and I can feel it flow deep down to my bones. It is those little trickles that keep me alive.

I can't explain this pain I feel in my chest every single day, every moment. It stings my eyes. It chokes my breath. It makes me feel sick in the pit of my stomach. Tears me from within. Rips me apart in a way that I can hear something snapping inside me. But you know what the good news is? In knowing pain, I feel I am beginning to know you.

I know I am supposed to be strong for you. I am holding up and carrying on, but I get weary sometimes—just a little.

Just take me along wherever you are going, will you? I want to walk with you all the way, till the end and beyond.

Life is short——I just had to say it while I still could.

Renu

Once she was done, she took a deep breath, read the letter slowly, crumpled the piece of paper and threw it into the bin. If there was one person in the world with whom she could share her thoughts uninhibitedly, it was herself.

EIGHTEEN

I have to go to Sitapur. I just have to go to Sitapur. I have to talk to Dev and put an end to all this. The thought pricked Renu's senses as soon as she opened her eyes in the morning. She had cast all her fears, all conventions aside, and loved Arjun from the depths of her soul. And her love had failed. Arjun could never be hers. In her longing for Arjun, she was even willing to let go what she had. Despite the unbearable heaviness in her heart, she knew she had to make it right. For the sake of her two children. Avi was sleeping right next to her, comfortably nestled in her arms. The innocence on his face put her inner turbulence to rest, even if for a short while. *What am I doing and why?*

She knew that she was as good as a single parent to her children by now. Dev was seldom around any more and as much as he was attached to the children, his involvement in their daily lives was almost nothing. With every passing day, she could sense Dev drifting further away from the family. He would rarely call, and even if he would, conversing with him would be a struggle. He seemed perpetually irritated and passive aggressive, but he always made sure to ask after Bauji.

She looked out of the door. The lights were on in Aneisha's room and her heart filled up with pride for her daughter. It was barely five in the morning and she was already up by herself, studying for her exams. Aneisha was growing up to be a responsible young woman.

Schools would close for the Dusshera holidays in a few days—that would be the perfect time to visit Dev in Sitapur. Renu was oddly looking forward to this particular trip. Was it her inner guilt that made her want to make everything all right? She wasn't sure. If nothing else, she thought it would at least be a change from her monotonous life. She would find the time away from family responsibilities and be able to speak to Dev. See for one last time what his reaction would be. She hadn't stepped out of the city in years and her mind was buckling under apprehensions. Dev's treatment of her had left her wary and forever fearful of rejection, but she knew she had to do this for her children. What she felt for Dev or what Dev felt for her did not matter any more. They were a family and the future of her children was at stake. She was acutely aware that she had faltered, but this was not the time to mull over the pain of heartbreak. She had to do everything in her power to pull her life back into normalcy.

But what about Bauji?

What about him, Renu?

Renu tiptoed her way out into the living area where
Bauji was sitting immersed in his newspapers. He flung an
angry glance at Renu, silently reprimanding her for being
late with his morning tea. Renu looked up at the wall clock
and it was seven already. How long had she been lying
around in bed?

This dissociation with the passage of time had become
an increasingly common occurrence. Time never seemed to
move in sync with her, or she with it. Normally, a situation
like this, however rare, would leave her flustered and even
guilty. Today, however, she felt different.

'Bauji, I have to go to Sitapur for a few days,' she said
coolly.

Her statement rendered the old man speechless for a
moment. 'Are you asking me or telling me?'

Renu wasn't quite sure what she should answer to that.
Maybe she should have put that across as a request, instead
of an announcement? Or maybe not.

'I have to go,' she said, a bit more assertively this
time. Bauji did not reply but the quiver of his lips and the
twitching in his facial muscles implied enough. 'Champa
will stay back during the day to look after you and the kids.
She knows everything and I will coordinate things with her
before I leave,' she said and made her way to the kitchen.
She felt slightly guilty that young Aneisha would have to fill
in for her the rest of the time because the old man couldn't
even fetch himself a glass of water to save his life, but she
drew solace from the fact that the children would be at
home for the Dusshera holidays, so there would be no stress

on that front. She had adequately briefed Aneisha without giving out too much, but Aneisha being Aneisha, had read a lot out of her mother's worried eyes.

'Is everything all right between you and Papa,' she had asked, to which Renu had replied in the affirmative, although unconvincingly. Aneisha had promised to look after Avi in Renu's absence and Renu knew she could trust her daughter with anything.

As she waited for the tea on the stove to bubble up, she quietly observed Bauji from the window opening up into the dining room. Even from that distance, she could make out the terse expression on his face and the seething rage in his eyes. He wasn't really reading the newspaper at that moment, just frantically flipping the pages and making a lot of noise in doing so, trying to make his displeasure known at her defiance.

A smirk of amusement spread across Renu's lips as she watched him try to deal with what had just happened and fail spectacularly. She knew he would call Dev to complain about her wayward behaviour, and she had to find a way to stop him.

As she put his tea on the table next to where he was sitting she spoke, 'I have one request, Bauji—please don't tell Dev that I am coming. I can't explain much at this stage but please understand that I am doing it for the sake of this family,' she said. 'Can I have your support on this, please?'

Regardless of Bauji's treatment of her, she was well aware of his commitment towards the family, especially his son. He nodded reluctantly, without letting go of his frown lines. Maybe, for once, he did sense the gravity of the situation from her tone.

~

Renu's mind wasn't really focused on the stuff she was hurriedly throwing into the suitcase. Her heart was gripped with a peculiar anxiety. She didn't know if she was doing the right thing by springing a surprise on Dev in Sitapur. She hadn't seen him in weeks, and the chasm between them appeared to be widening with every passing day.

She knew where he lived, she had been to his place once. It was a small one-bedroom apartment in a building, just big enough for a single person. Renu had never really lived there with him, except for the time when she had gone over a weekend to help him settle down, back when Dev had just moved to Sitapur.

When the train pulled up at the Sitapur railway station, Renu was filled with equal parts of hurt and hope. Even though she had stood up to him, deep in her chest she still felt the after-ache of her last letter to Arjun. *Maybe this is a sign*, she consoled herself. Maybe it was the universe telling her that she had faltered and strayed from the right path, and that it was now time to go back home. Dev was her home. Dev meant safety, security and stability.

As her auto rickshaw made its way through the narrow cluttered streets of Sitapur, the dust, the noise and the unruly traffic threatened to overwhelm Renu, but her mind was preoccupied with what she would say to Dev. Would he be happy or shocked to see her here? She seldom did anything without his permission or approval, let alone travel all the way from Lucknow to meet him here by herself. For Renu, this felt like the only chance to salvage what was left of their marriage. It would be easier to connect with Dev, she thought, away from home and the kids, and most importantly, Bauji. Dev hadn't been quite himself on his visits to Lucknow, and she had put it down to stress and the burden of responsibilities on his shoulders. Here, in Sitapur, they would be alone. Just the two of them. Perhaps it was just the right environment to talk about their differences and work out a way ahead. She had made a mistake with Arjun, and she was ready to bury it deep within her heart. Even his memories, however painful they may be, and make a fresh start with Dev. That was the only right thing to do; for her own self as well as for her family. She had been selfish enough to chase what wasn't destined for her, and she wanted to make up for it with whatever she had.

Her fingers trembled a little as she rang the doorbell and she took a deep breath to calm her nervously pounding heart.

'Yes?' She was greeted by a woman. A rather familiar-looking woman.

Shock quickly gave way to disorientation and confusion as Renu struggled to make sense of things around her. In a flash, the woman's face, which had turned into a blurry haze, finally found a match in her memory. She was Kamini, an upcoming author, two of whose books had been published by Ravenhouse. Renu had never met her in person, but she remembered her from the photographs in newspapers and

posters at Ravenhouse Publishers during the much-hyped
celebrity launch of her debut novel. The book hadn't sold
much but being the daughter of a rich businessman, Kamini
had spent quite a sum in projecting herself as the *next best
thing in the world of publishing*.

'Kamini?' Renu blurted out awkwardly as soon as she
managed to partially gather her wits.

'What do you want?' Kamini demanded haughtily. The
confidence in her voice irked Renu. The woman in front
of her had obviously not recognized her. A fleeting thought
crossed Renu's mind, 'Am I at the wrong house?' but a
look at the wall behind Kamini erased all doubts. On the
wall of the living room, right behind Kamini, was a painting
made by Aneisha.

'I am Dev's wife. Renu. And you need to tell me what
you're doing here in my husband's house!' she demanded.
By now the confusion in her mind had given way to anger.

'Hahaha! Renu? Or, Maya?' Even though Renu was
stunned into silence, Kamini seemed absolutely unfazed,
almost as if she was expecting Renu to drop in and find her
there. To say that Kamini's question shocked and rattled
Renu, would have been an understatement. She braced
herself for what was to unfold.

Something did not feel right and a lot of it did not
add up.

'You do know that Dev is married, right?' Renu feared
the worst and a million possibilities crossed her mind in that
moment. She wasn't sure what to make of the smug look in
Kamini's eyes and the latter's silence wasn't helping.

'Of course, I do. But he loves me.'

'You're lying!' Renu stammered disbelievingly.

'Dev will be home any moment. Why don't you talk to him yourself?' Kamini leaned against the door with a hand placed on her hip.

Renu heard footsteps behind her and turned around to find Dev walking up the stairs. He froze in his tracks when he saw the two women standing at the doorstep.

NINETEEN

'Renu! What are you doing here?' Dev's expression was a mix of shock and guilt when he saw the two women standing at his doorstep.

'I came here to see you,' Renu replied, hurt and shock evident in her voice. There was a lot she wanted to say to Dev but she was not sure if she had the voice or the words left for it. She didn't have the face to accuse Dev of cheating on her when she herself had strayed.

'Can we talk for a while?' Dev asked politely, a little disconcerted by Renu's calmness.

'Kamini, will you please . . .'

Kamini made her way into the bedroom without saying a word and Dev signalled to Renu to sit on the sofa in the living room. Renu looked around the house, for the first time since last year. It did not look like a bachelor's pad any more. The living room had been done up tastefully, with an elegant sofa set and colour-coordinated curtains. There were a few paintings on the walls, a lamp in the corner and a vase with artificial flowers to add some colour to the décor. This was not how she remembered leaving the house. The realization that it was Kamini who had made her husband's barren house a home pinched her but she didn't utter a word.

Instead, she looked at Dev expectantly, hoping he'd say something to help her make sense of the bizarre situation. From what it looked like, her marriage, or whatever was left of it, was beyond salvation of any kind, but she still wanted to hear his side of the story.

And he told her. Just the way it had happened, not holding back anything . . .

~

'That book in your hand . . .' the woman pointed as she tried to strike a conversation. Dev sat on the seat right opposite her in the train. It was a second class air-conditioned coach and was almost empty, leaving just the two of them in that compartment.

Dev had barely started reading before the woman had him engaged in a conversation. 'What about it?' he asked. Until now, he hadn't really looked up but the woman's sweet feminine voice caught his attention. She was petite, with striking brown eyes and shoulder-length hair that engulfed her face in wild curls. Her jeans and fitted kurti beautifully framed her slender, toned body and Dev found it increasingly difficult to keep his eyes off her.

'How do you feel about it?'

Dev looked down at the cover, wondering if his gaze had made the lady uncomfortable. *Kiss of a Stranger* by Maya. His face flushed a little out of embarrassment. He wasn't much of a reader but there were a few authors whose books he did not miss. Maya was one of them.

'I've read all of Maya's books. I find her fascinating,' he said after a short pause. This woman was a stranger. What did he have to lose?

'Fascinating?' Kamini raised an eyebrow.

'Yes. Her mind. Her thoughts. She writes boldly and fearlessly, like nobody is going to read what she's written. She must be a fascinating woman. I have never come across anyone like her . . .' his voice trailed off.

The woman smiled.

'Can you keep a secret if I tell you one?' Kamini asked seductively.

'Yes, of course,' Dev replied awkwardly. He wasn't very used to conversing with women, especially women like the one sitting in front of him. It had been years since he had had any interaction with a woman apart from Renu. And Renu was mellow, nowhere close to the confident diva that this woman seemed to be. Not only was she beautiful, she had a compelling aura about her and a voice that was hard to ignore.

Her eyes penetrated deep into Dev's, telling him what she wanted without using any words.

'What secret?' Dev tried to veer back to their conversation. It had only been a few minutes since they had met and it had to be a play of destiny for them to be seated next to each other on that train from Lucknow to Sitapur. Dev had been enraptured by this woman at first sight but he was aware that she was way out of his league. But now, her eyes told a different story. He didn't know how to respond.

'I am Maya. I wrote this book,' she whispered even though there was no one around to eavesdrop.

Dev's heart skipped a beat. *Was this happening for real?* He found himself tongue-tied and almost incapacitated.

'Is that your real name? Maya?' he stammered.

'No, my real name is Kamini. I write under the pseudonym, Maya. Here's my card,' she offered. Sure enough, it had her name, Kamini Oberoi, with the logo of Ravenhouse Publishers right underneath. Dev started at it blankly for a few moments.

'Aren't you going to tell me your name?' she asked sweetly.

'Dev. My name is Dev,' he stuttered. 'I'm just a regular guy though, not a celebrity like you,' he added awkwardly.

'I'm very glad we met, Dev. You seem like an interesting person.'

Dev almost blushed. He had been called a few things in his life, but *interesting* certainly wasn't one of them. His existence was as ordinary as could be, and for him, the woman sitting in front of him was larger than life.

'If you don't mind, can I ask you something, Maya? Sorry, Kamini . . .'

'I think we are friends now. You can ask me anything you want.'

'Why don't you write as yourself? I mean, as Kamini? You are so talented,' he gushed. His heartbeat had almost stabilized by now as the moment had sunk in. He was indeed conversing with Maya, the woman who had dominated his fantasies ever since he chanced upon and read her first book.

'Oh, Dev! You know how our society is. If my family found out that I write such stories, they will kill me. Sometimes, I feel very scared!' she said.

'I can understand. I wish people understood talent. You are a brave woman, Kamini. I really admire you for your courage,' he said with a smile and Kamini smiled back coyly.

'Mine is a lonely existence, Dev. Despite all the success, I have no one to call my own. No one who would understand me. These words are all I have . . .' Kamini said forlornly and trailed off. 'I'm sorry. I didn't mean to bore you with all this. I usually don't open up to strangers like this. I don't know why . . .' she added after a few moments.

'Please keep going. I like listening to you talk,' Dev said.

'Do you feel the same way, Dev? Tell me honestly.'

'Feel what way?'

'Lonely. Anchorless. Drifting. Bored of a mundane existence. As if you are playing multiple roles but your life has no meaning because you lost your real self somewhere along the way?'

'Hmm. I guess everyone feels that way sometimes. It's a part of life,' Dev explained matter-of-factly.

'But does it have to be this way? Imagine how beautiful life could be if we had someone to love, someone who loved us back for who we really are, deeply connected with our souls. It wouldn't seem so dreary then, would it?'

'I don't know, I guess you are right,' Dev shrugged. Dev had never given these things a thought. It wasn't like him to analyse and daydream of possibilities that he knew were out of his reach. He wasn't entirely happy with his existence, but he had made peace with it. He had learnt the art of being content. Kamini's words got him thinking.

'Do you want me to read a passage from the book for you?' she asked, finding him deep in thought.

'Please do. It will be my privilege.' It was an offer Dev didn't want to refuse; to hear the words of his favourite author in her own voice, sitting right next to her. It was almost like he was in a dream-like trance.

Kamini got up from her seat to sit next to Dev. The subtle fragrance of her floral perfume permeated his nostrils as she took the book from his hands and began flipping the pages. Their physical proximity had already got him feeling heady.

'She opened up like a flower for him and he filled her body with the sensation of a bee sting. She lost herself in his embrace, surrendered and satiated.

'They didn't realize when their souls found each other, as their hands and mouths explored hidden corners of their bodies. And to think it had all started with an innocent kiss. A stranger's kiss.'

Kamini looked up from the page to decipher the expression on Dev's face. His nervousness grew with the quivering of her moist lips, as did his urge to sweep her in his arms and see for himself what they tasted like.

The moment he was in was far out of reach of his wildest fantasies, yet it was unfolding before him magically in the most beautiful manner. He wanted to savour every drop of it before someone shook him awake from this beautiful dream. Kamini, however, wasn't one to be held back by hesitation. She swirled her fingers around the back of his neck and kissed him like he'd never been kissed before.

'So how did you like the *kiss of a stranger*, hmm?' Kamini asked.

The train was about to pull up at the Sitapur station and they both knew what was to follow.

What Dev had not anticipated was that this seemingly casual tryst with Kamini wouldn't end up being a one-off encounter. They began meeting often and before he knew it, she had made her way into his life and his heart, and eventually, his home. In her, he saw a fire that he never found in Renu. She brought a freshness to his drab existence. She wasn't an obligation or a responsibility, but a companion. She was the perfect escape, and a beautiful one at that . . .

~

Renu heard him out, then asked, 'What should we do now, Dev?'

'Listen, Renu. There is no better way to say this, but I love Kamini,' Dev responded quickly as if to get the weight off his chest.

However, the heaviness lingered in the air between them as Renu soaked in his words. To her surprise, they didn't break her the way she thought they would, but they did make the ground under her feet tremble a little.

'And our children? What about them?' she said, blurting out the first thought that came to her mind. She knew very well that from here on, her life was about to change and that nothing could go back to being the same, even though it was never a great life to begin with. Her entire existence had centred around Dev, the kids and their home for a long time, till Arjun came into her life, and suddenly, she felt every single thing slipping away like sand from between her fingers. The stable foundation of a home that she had built her life on was now crumbling under the weight of uncertainty. If Dev chose to leave her, where would she go and what would she do? She had nothing and no one in the whole wide world apart from this family to call her own. Her worst fears were coming true—her life had come a full circle and she was about to reach the same place from where she had started. The place of terrifying loneliness and insecurity.

'I am still their father, and your husband. My family is still my responsibility,' he replied stoically. He kept gazing at the painting on the wall opposite to where he sat. While his voice remained unfaltering, he refused to look at her in the eye as he spoke.

Renu wasn't sure how she felt about living with Bauji and tending to the house, all the while knowing that her husband was living with another woman. But, she had stepped out of the boundaries of marriage too, and given herself to Arjun. How could she now point fingers at Dev?

'But why? How?' she stammered, unable to put her barrage of questions in a sequence. She wanted to know what Kamini had to offer to Dev that she did not. Was he happy with her? Of course, he was. His dwindling presence from their home and their lives was proof enough.

Dev, on the other hand, didn't display any signs of guilt or remorse. He probably didn't consider it necessary to explain himself and his decisions to his wife, the mother of his children. It was enough that he wasn't abandoning them and would continue to support them financially. He just kept averting his eyes from her. His stony silence told her that he had sailed too far away from the shore. For him, she was no more than a liability—someone he had to fend for because he had promised to. *She was a burden.*

Renu's mind was in a strange place between exploding chaos and eerie dark blankness. She once again swept her gaze across the room and that's when she spotted a stack of books on the side table—all of them Maya's.

TWENTY

It had been a couple of weeks since Renu's return from Sitapur. As she coped with the storms brewing outside of her and within, she carried on with her responsibilities in stoic silence. Nothing seemed to move her any more—not Bauji's acidic tongue, not her children's innocent chatter. An all-consuming confusion had taken over her life.

'Mrs Kumar, could you please spare some time to come over? It's important.' It was a cold winter morning when Renu received a call from Aneisha's school. The principal's voice was low and sullen.

Renu's felt something sinking in her chest. 'Are Aneisha and Avi okay?' she stammered nervously.

'Yes, yes, they are absolutely fine, Mrs Kumar. I just wanted to discuss Aneisha's performance with you,' the principal replied, suddenly aware that she might have pushed a panic button with her seemingly stern tone.

Renu breathed a sigh of relief. Aneisha had always been an independent girl and an exceptionally bright student. It was probably nothing to worry about but nevertheless, she decided to leave the house immediately. If she reached on time, she could pick up the kids and bring them back with her.

The school was a good 15 kilometres away, in Aliganj. It was one of the best schools in the city and it was with great difficulty that Dev and Renu had managed to get admission in it for the children. The fees were a little more than they could fairly afford, but then, they did not want to compromise on the quality of the children's education. The school bus took the children back and forth, but today Renu decided that she would take the children out for lunch at McDonald's. *They would be so thrilled!* She thought to herself and smiled. It had been ages since she had taken the children out anywhere. In fact, they went out as a family only when Dev was in town, which was getting increasingly rarer. She often longed to take both kids for a fun outing but with Bauji at home, the idea never worked out. Today was just the perfect opportunity.

Renu reached school half an hour before the final bell and headed straight to the principal's office. Mrs Nigam, a short, portly lady in her forties, stood up to greet her before gesturing her to sit. She made a quick call through the intercom to summon Aneisha's class teacher who arrived into the office within minutes.

'Good afternoon, Mrs Jose,' Renu wished the lady as she took a seat beside the principal at the other end of the table. Renu had interacted with Mrs Jose several times before during parent–teacher meetings and the latter had always been very impressed with Aneisha's consistently good academic performances. In fact, a couple of months ago, Aneisha had been appointed the school prefect, a title that she was extremely proud of.

Renu watched the two women as they exchanged glances, and the terse expression on their faces perturbed her a little. 'Is everything all right, Mrs Jose?' she asked.

'Mrs Kumar, I wanted to discuss Aneisha's performance and her conduct at school with you,' Mrs Jose took a deep breath as she prepared to speak. Renu could almost feel her heart in her throat.

'Is everything okay?' she repeated.

'Well, frankly, I am very concerned about your daughter. Her performance has been plummeting over the past few weeks. We thought of calling you since these years are crucial for her. She hardly pays attention in class lately, her assignments are never complete and her grades are dipping drastically.'

'Oh, but she has always been a good student . . .' Renu muttered, unsure whether she was talking to herself, or the two women sitting on the other side of the table.

'Can I ask you something, Mrs Kumar? And will you reply honestly?'

'Sure.'

'Is everything all right at home? I mean, in the family? Children often get perturbed when there is any kind of disharmony in their environment,' Mrs Jose's eyes probed Renu questioningly.

'No, Mrs Jose. There's nothing of the sort. Everything is normal at home,' Renu replied. 'I'll talk to Aneisha and find out what's wrong. I assure you she'll be back to her potential soon.'

'We hope so too,' Mrs Nigam added with a comforting smile.

Renu thanked the two teachers and got up to leave.

'There's something else too,' Mrs Nigam added, looking at Mrs Jose, urging her to take over. Renu sank back into her seat, once again flooded with anxiety.

'Mrs Kumar, I don't know how to put this across and I don't know how you'll take it but the class prefect saw Aneisha on the stairs with a boy . . .' her voice trailed off.

'What do you mean? Please speak clearly,' Renu's voice had a touch of defensiveness and aggression. Aneisha was only sixteen. What were the teachers trying to imply? It was normal for teenagers to be curious about the opposite sex, but . . .

'You are wise, Mrs Kumar. You know what I mean,' Mrs Jose replied. She seemed concerned about Aneisha but Renu had become totally oblivious to that. She hauled herself up from the chair and with heavy steps, walked out of the office.

What had sparked of as a seething rage, denatured into an ominous guilt. By the time Renu reached home and bolted the door of the room behind her, she was ready to break down. *All this has happened because of me! I've neglected my children!* It was overpowering and all too consuming, this guilt. She had been so wound up in chasing her desires that she hadn't noticed what her daughter might be going through. Aneisha, all of sixteen, was a brilliant student, a sensible and a grounded child. She had her whole life ahead of her.

In her daze, Renu hadn't even bothered to pick up the children from school. They would come back in the school bus, like every day. Leave alone taking them out for lunch, Renu wasn't even sure how she would face her own daughter. A part of her was angry, for how could her daughter, who she had been brought up so well, do something so stupid and tarnish her own reputation in school? Another part of her understood, but was terribly weighed down by the guilt of failing her children and not being there to hold her daughter's hand in this most challenging phase in her life so far.

TWENTY-ONE

Renu had been waiting for this day for an entire week and every moment in the lead up had weighed down heavily upon her. It was a Saturday and Dev had promised to come home. It was time to tell him her truth. The truth she had hidden from everyone for years and the truth that had now been overshadowed by Kamini's lies. She didn't know what Kamini was up to, but in Dev's eyes, she had seen admiration for Maya. At first she had let it go and let Kamini be Maya. But it was affecting their lives. Their children needed a stable home, which right now it wasn't. And maybe she had been wrong about Dev. Maybe he would accept her for who she was, and probably love her like he loved Kamini.

The events that had transpired in Sitapur had sent her reeling in shock and hurt, but it had also planted a bud of hope in her heart. If Dev was enamoured of Kamini because he thought she was Maya, maybe it wouldn't be so difficult to turn that around in her favour. She had all the evidence that Kamini didn't—her manuscripts, her correspondence with editors, fan mail and most of all, the royalty cheques.

The flutter of optimism made Renu a bit impatient as she heard Dev's car pull into the driveway. She would take him straight to their bedroom and tell him everything. She rushed outside to greet him, but to her disappointment, Bauji had got there before her. She watched them from a distance as Bauji handed Dev an envelope, a stoic expression on his face.

In an instant, she saw Dev's face transform and become contorted with rage.

She had never seen him this angry before. Despite everything, Dev had, for the most part, been a calm person. It took a lot to get him worked up to that level of anger.

'What is it, Dev?' Renu asked, rushing towards him, as he entered their room.

In response, he hurled the rectangular envelope in her direction viciously. From the logo in the bottom-left corner, she could make out that it was a correspondence from Ravenhouse Publishers, and her heart sank. She looked into Dev's fiery eyes waiting for him to speak up as she picked the envelope to inspect its contents. Inside it was a cheque of Rs 50,000 addressed in Renu's name. It was the same cheque Renu had collected from the office a few days ago and had forgotten to deposit at the bank. Seemed like Bauji had found it.

'Since how long have you been fooling us?' asked Dev in a chilling voice so low that it rattled her insides. She'd meant to tell him everything but not like this. She had no explanation or justification for this parallel life she had been leading, but she'd decided to walk this last mile teetering on the hope that Dev would understand and accept her for who she was. That is why she had been waiting impatiently for him.

When she had returned from Sitapur, she had looked at things differently. Dev had openly professed his love for Kamini, but at the same time, Renu was aware that his relationship with Kamini was built upon a lie. Somewhere deep inside, she hoped that just as Arjun's truth had shattered all her illusions, Kamini's truth would shake Dev out of his spell. This was certainly not how she'd envisioned it would turn out to be.

'Dev, please don't be angry. I was going to tell you everything . . .'

'Since how long?' Dev bellowed and pushed aside a chair so it crashed onto the ground. Renu's insides trembled with fear but she didn't let that show in case it angered him even more. This wasn't the time to lose composure.

Renu scuttled over to the kitchen and fetched a glass of cool water for her husband. 'Here, drink this. Let's talk about this. It's nothing like you think,' she pleaded.

Dev refused the water, so she gently placed the glass on the table and sat down on a chair opposite him. His nostrils were flared, she could see and his chest heaving under his strained breathing. There would be questions. Endless questions. And she would have to answer each one of them. She would have to face the truth and so would he. She knew it wasn't going to be easy.

'I write because I like writing, Dev,' Renu began in a soft voice. 'And, I am Maya. Kamini isn't.' Her eyes hung low and there was a tinge of apology in her voice.

'What? What are you saying? You are Maya? How could you, Renu? How could you? You didn't think of us even once? Me, Bauji, the kids?'

Even though he knew her truth, he seemed to feel the shock of her words.

'I'm tired of hiding now, Dev. I don't want you to live a life of lies. I saw how much adulation you have for Kamini but with me, you . . .'

'Really? You like writing this filthy porn?' Dev replied sharply, looking straight at her. Anger was dripping from his eyes and Renu fumbled to find the right words to calm him down. 'Did you not think for even a single moment what the society will think of us? Think of you? Did you even once think how Aneisha and Avinash would feel when they come to know that their mother is a cheap porn writer? We may not have much, Renu, but we are a respected family. And you are all set to destroy it by telling the world what filth goes on in your mind!'

Renu felt something stir within her core. Filth? Her words were *filth*? Her creativity was *filth*. Her desires were *filth*. *She* was filth?

Dev's hypocrisy astounded her and she felt rage boiling inside her like hot lava, ready to explode. Kamini was the woman of his dreams, while she was a disgrace to the family!

Don't say anything, Renu. Don't . . .

'That's why I used a pen name . . .' she whispered, not convinced with her words. Her family's reputation wasn't the reason she had chosen to write as Maya. She had chosen Maya because she wanted to break away from her identity, to think freely, to write freely, without any shackles of culture, propriety and tradition to hold her down. She wanted to express herself the way she was, not the way her family or society expected her to be.

'I never thought that you of all people would end up writing such cheap, dirty books. For what, Renu? What for?'

And then it exploded out of her.

'For myself! I write for myself! I write to express myself. I write to give wings to my fantasies. I write to be known. To be read. To be admired. To tell stories. I write for the same reason every writer writes. And these are the same cheap filthy books you buy and read in secrecy! These are the same cheap books that titillate your fantasies. I am the same Maya you are so enamoured with. The same dirty-minded slut who shamed your family, the same seductress that haunts the deepest, darkest corners of your mind!' By now Renu was shaking with anger. She couldn't believe Dev's reaction. 'Tell me truthfully, Dev, haven't you ever wondered how it would feel like to be in bed with a woman who thinks like that? A woman full of passion and desire waiting to be unleashed? That's what drew you to Kamini, isn't it?'

'With Kamini, it is different. She's not my wife or the mother of my children,' Dev stated matter-of-factly. Renu laughed so loud that her voice echoed across the house, and she laughed till her sides hurt. She stood away from him, alone. And then she said the words she never thought she would say to the father of her children. 'Goodbye, Dev.'

Dev stood there looking at her, paralysed in shock.

This wasn't like Renu at all. He had known her for years, or at least he thought he did. Who was this woman? There were a million parallel thoughts buzzing in his mind, leaving him perplexed. His wife's secret life. Kamini's lies and betrayal. He had no clue what was going on and why. He knew he had been cheating all along on Renu, but he felt cheated too. By both the women in his life.

TWENTY-TWO

'You should be happy, I am with you. Close to you.'

A warm tear rolled down Renu's cheek. She was going through a turbulent time. Even though love was dead long ago, her separation from Dev was taking its toll on her. She was still living in the same house with Bauji and the children but it was only a matter of time before she would have to move out, once the legal proceedings were completed. Dev hadn't resisted the idea of a divorce at all, it was almost as if he had wanted it himself. She had realized that the way her husband was wired, he would never accept her as Maya, while on the other hand he would happily live with a mistress who had lied to him about her identity. She didn't need all this in her life any more and her relationship with Arjun wasn't bringing her any solace either.

Conversations with Arjun were increasingly becoming a tug of war. It was as if she was walking on eggshells all the time, fearful and anxious of saying or doing something that would annoy him and make him flinch from her. She had found such beauty and contentment with Arjun that she couldn't let him go, not even when he kept rejecting her disdainfully when he pleased. She had surrendered her entire being to him and she clung on to those illusions like her life depended on them, knowing fully well that they were just that—illusions.

But that's a fascinating thing about the human mind— reality can never match up to the magnificence of illusions. They are so pure, so perfect and so real, even if just in our heads, that we are willing to risk our whole lives and existence to bask in them just one more time, every time. Such is our hunger and greed for perfect love and beauty, that we chase this mirage unto the end—our end.

There was so much she wanted to tell him, so much she wanted to make him understand. Overwhelmed by the surge of emotions building up inside her, she decided to lay herself bare before him—one last time. She wasn't sure if her words would have any effect on him, though.

For my Arjun,
It hurts even more now when you come close. Your touch always comes with a bitter reminder that it is fleeting and that it will be gone the moment I believe it is here to stay. Just as quickly as you make me feel warm, I know you will leave me cold and fragmented.

For you Arjun, I ignore what is so clearly visible and glaring in my eyes. The woman in me can be blind but my art is not. The writer in me observes like she should, makes mental notes as she should, interprets realities as she should, and writes the truth as it is. I used to believe that writers are capable of telling the most beautiful lies but that's not true. Writers express truths that are difficult to swallow. Hence, most are disguised as fiction. Fiction is just fact with lots of make-up on so that it looks unrecognizably beautiful.

It is the woman in me who is weak and unwilling to drop the beautiful glittery gossamer shrouding your truth because what waits to be seen is so ugly that it will shatter me into a million deaths. It will shatter my perception of myself and my confidence in my intellect. It will make me doubt my intuition and prove me wrong before my own eyes. And how, after swallowing the truth, will I be able to look you in the eye? In a split second, you will fall from grace in my eyes and turn into the cold, conniving, heartless beast you actually are. I will lose all my love for you—this pure love that I have never felt for anyone before. I will lose it all in the blink of an eye. And I may never be able to feel this way again. What if I am never able to feel this way again, Arjun?

You were my journey into myself. You were more than a scar—you were every scar. You brought to life all my fears, all my fallacies, you unleashed my madness all over again, you pinned me to a wall and forced me to stare at my demons in the eye. I don't know if I could do the same for you. I hope I did. I think I did.

And into that journey into myself, I also met many beautiful strangers. Some who broke my fall, some who walked with me, fought with me, held my hand, held me. But ultimately I realized that there are some journeys you have to take on your own. Some paths you have to tread with no hand to hold, even if it is dark and riddled with thorns. It was scary, yes, but it was the only way forward.

Our relationship was full of turmoil but in your presence I also found peace.

You gave me many reasons to quit but my soul had only one reason to stay—and that reason was you. I couldn't leave you for the world. But you could, so easily. Every single time. You have given me enough pain to last a lifetime. How are you going to compensate for that?

Yours,
Renu

Renu's eyes pried Arjun's when he looked up from the piece of paper.

'You are going bloody insane. Go see a doctor,' he said coldly.

'Yes, the insanity that bothers you so is the same insanity with which I've loved you and you're taking that away from me.'

'GODDAMIT, Renu! What have I done to you?'

'What have you done? I can tell you what you have done, provided you have the courage to hear me out before walking away!'

'Tell me!'

'You took me up into the clouds and then dropped me on a bed of shattered glass. You stripped me bare of my dignity, my self-respect and my worth and trampled all over me. You stabbed me with your words and left countless wounds on my soul, which will fester forever. And then, when I was at my weakest, you dealt me your last blow because I did not have anything more to give to you. You left me destroyed and broken, and yet here I am, trying to prove my strength to you—or rather to myself—when in reality, I don't have any left. I am trying frantically and desperately for that last twig of hope that would keep me from sinking, knowing fully well that it will take more than a twig to keep me afloat. But do you know what my real doom is? I am fighting the wrong battle. Not even a losing battle, just the wrong battle!'

Arjun just sat there, staring blankly at Maya. She hadn't meant to raise her voice but she was indeed falling apart. She took a few deep breaths, till her heartbeat returned to normal. It was her idea to meet outside the house, in a resort a little away from the city so that they could talk peacefully.

She had struggled way too much, all alone, and she was exhausted down to her soul. Something within her told her that it was time to let go. Of everything.

They sat beside each other in quietude as white pigeons trotted across the green lawn. The garden swing rocked gently but the confusion erupting in Renu's heart was no baby that could be swayed into a slumber. Her fingers gingerly tiptoed towards Arjun and locked themselves in the spaces between his. She squeezed his palm, but his remained limp. He looked at her, and she tried reading his eyes—stony and blank, without any emotion in them. Hers, on the other hand were teaming with questions, hurt, anger and pain, and tears. Arjun had not considered it worth his while to even respond to her outburst and in his silence Renu had found all her answers.

It is rightly said, the opposite of love is not hate. It is indifference. It is not the lack of love that kills. It is the lies, the deceit, the unending mind games and the wounds inflicted on the soul that kill—a slow, painful death. And yet, we don't give up on love. We trudge on, with the faint, dimming, flickering light of hope in our already shattered heart. Because if hope kills, the lack of it kills faster.

TWENTY–THREE

It had been over three hours since Renu had been staring at the blank word document on the screen. There was so much noise in her head, so much to express but all fragmented and disjointed. Loss of inspiration or a sensory overload of emotions, she couldn't decide but her thoughts frequently rebelled against her and refused to flow out like a smooth river, like they did before.

'Renu! There is something very important I have to tell you. Can you please come and meet me?'

'What's wrong, Akriti?' The panic in Akriti's voice was palpable, and it certainly wasn't like her to get so worked up unless there was something majorly wrong.

'I can't tell you over the phone. You will have to meet me!' she insisted frantically. Renu had no option but to agree. She asked Akriti to come to a café near her house so that she could sneak out easily for a few minutes after lunch when Bauji took his nap.

Akriti looked flustered when she entered the cafe and took a seat opposite Renu in the corner of the small coffee shop. It was unbearably hot outside so the place was fairly devoid of people. 'I am sorry for calling you out like this but I really had to talk to you right now!' Akriti panted.

'Relax, Akriti. Sit down first, catch your breath and have some water. There's plenty of time to talk,' Renu said calmly, pouring a glass of water from the jug for her friend.

'Did you share your manuscript with Kamini?' Akriti asked directly without mincing any words. Renu was taken aback. She couldn't make any sense of where this was coming from.

'Which manuscript?'

'The one titled "Maya"?'

Renu's heart sank to the pit of her stomach. 'No. Why? What happened?' she asked.

'Well, that book is being published by Ravenhouse under Kamini's name!'

'What! But how did Kamini . . .'

'I don't know how she got hold of your draft, which is why I asked if you had shared it with her? The moment I read the manuscript, I knew it was yours.'

'Does Arjun know about this?' Renu asked in a low voice, her heart thumping wildly, hoping against hope that what she was imagining was not true. Arjun would never do that to her . . .

'Arjun? What has Arjun got to do with this? Of course he knows! And he has a grand marketing plan in place for the book's release at the Lit Fest.'

Renu felt the blood drain from her head. 'Are you all right?' Akriti asked, holding her by the shoulder and shaking her up.

'I don't really know, Akriti . . .' she managed to mumble.

'I just want to know how did Kamini get her hands on your manuscript?'

'I had shared it with Arjun,' Renu confessed, remembering that evening when Arjun had thrown a childlike tantrum to get her to share the manuscript with him. She looked Akriti in the eye. She did not have to say anything else. Akriti was smart enough to piece the fragments together.

The two women sat in silence for a while, in the same spot yet in different zones. Akriti, flabbergasted and unable to decide what to make of the situation, and Renu, heartbroken with yet another knife plunged down her heart. She had so far endured every wound that Arjun had inflicted on her, believed every lie, swallowed all the pain but now it had peaked. The bitter scent of betrayal filled up her senses and she heard the silent shatter of her heart ringing through her ears. Her lips curled into a comfortable smile, most naturally while the unbearable turmoil ripped her soul apart.

Her thoughts slowly started ebbing from the darkness of pain and grief and found their way to the white hot zone of rage—the space where revenge is born.

Since that meeting with Akriti, things changed for her. Even if there was a dim flicker of hope with Arjun, it was now dead. Nothing could break her further, for she had nothing left to lose.

Every night she would lie all alone in bed, in the silence of the night, and battle her own soul. Her demons would poke her, prod her and instigate her to fight. Most times, she would turn her back to them, too exhausted to even think. At other times, she would indulge them and battle them, albeit with a weary soul. For a moment, she would think she had them tamed and wrapped around her fingers, but the very next moment, they would collectively overpower her and drag her down deep into an abyss. They would suffocate her with their weight, making it difficult for her to breathe. And yet, every morning, as the sun rose, she would pull herself out of the abyss, step out with a smile on her face and wave goodbye to her children as they boarded the school bus.

TWENTY-FOUR

It was one of the most difficult decisions she would make, but at the same time, the most liberating. It would have been easier if Dev was a scumbag, but unfortunately he wasn't, not like Arjun anyway. Renu knew the price of freedom—it was a heavy one. So many lives were at stake. Her world, which she had built slowly, brick-by-brick, over the years, was at stake. She was forgoing the safety and stability of her nest for the skies. Skies she had wistfully gazed at for years, and yet knew nothing about how it would feel to spread her wings and fly into the unknown. What would be the perils? What unknown dangers would it bring? Would she find what she had so long been looking for? She did not have the answers yet, but she also knew that the only way to find them was to take that leap of faith.

She was about to break all chains and shackles that had kept her grounded to her existence. All attachments, all relationships and all commitments. Yet, there were two people she could never let go of—Aneisha and Avi. From where she stood, it seemed like the end of the road for her, and she found herself standing on shaky ground. The last time she had felt this way was when her parents were separating, and once again, she felt like that lost and anchorless little girl. 'Please give me a sign, god . . .' she whispered out into the universe before she closed her teary eyes that night.

And that very moment god decided to hear her.

'Hello, is this Renu Mishra?' came a voice from the other end of the phone. It was another regular morning at the Kumar household and Renu was going about her business as usual. She had barely settled down with a cup of tea after sending the children off to school when the phone rang. It wasn't a familiar number.

'Yes?' she replied.

'Good morning, madam. I am Advocate Pramod Gupta from Lucknow High Court. I wanted to speak to you regarding some property rights.'

'Property rights? I don't own any property, Mr Gupta. I think you've got the wrong person,' she said.

'You are Mrs Komal Mishra's daughter, right?'

Renu stayed silent for a moment as the blurry image of her mother's face flashed before her eyes. It had been long. Way too long. She had almost forgotten that she had parents. What could her mother want from her now?

'Yes,' she replied in a shaky voice.

'Madam, I am sorry to tell you that your mother passed away a few months ago. She has left a few properties in your name. You will have to come over and sign some papers to take over them.'

Renu felt a lump build up in her throat. She barely remembered what her mother looked like, and yet, the news of her demise felt heavy on her chest. A solitary tear rolled down her cheek like a pearl drop. Her mother had left behind her assets for her. Her mother had been thinking of her! She could no longer ask her mother why she never came to meet her while she was still alive, but the thought that she was not a forgotten child, brought along with it a strange catharsis. A tinge of happiness in a moment of grief. A release. A letting go.

Providence might have taken its time to show her a path, but now it was there all right. She was now sure of what she wanted to do.

TWENTY–FIVE

Arjun looked into the mirror and his weary, battered self stared back at him. Never had he felt so defeated in his life. Never had a woman, a breed he had so loathed, and yet was helplessly addicted to, dared to get one up over him. He was Arjun. Arjun Singh Chauhan.

'The whore! She played me!' he yelled out aloud.

'You played her, Arjun. You knew she was a storm. You should've known better than to stir her.'

Arjun looked around the room. There was no one. The voice was coming from within.

It was true. Renu had decimated him to bits. The reputation and success of his publishing house had so far rested almost solely on the popularity of her books. Of course they published other titles, but none of them could match up to the frenzy and sales that came with the brand called 'Maya'. And now, not only had she taken that away from him, she had set him up for destruction and pinned him to a spot from where there was no escape. He was trapped, imprisoned.

The publishing house had invested lakhs in the publishing and marketing of Kamini's release, which was actually Maya's work. 25,000 copies were already printed and were lying in the warehouse. Press releases had been sent out when everything unravelled.

'How the hell did she come to know?' Kamini shrieked over the phone on learning about the fiasco.

'I have no idea. All I know is that we're over. This is the end,' Arjun replied.

He picked up a book lying on the table, and just reading the title made him seethe from within.

There, on a glossy paper coloured bright, bold red against a background of a silhouette of a seductress, were four letters embossed in an aesthetic black font—MAYA. On the side was a logo of a rival publishing firm.

Maya had sold off her latest book to another publishing house and timed the release carefully enough to leave Arjun with no escape route.

Not releasing the book would mean running into monetary losses from which a small-time publisher like him could never possibly recover, and releasing it would bring an end to whatever he had managed to build over the years. Not to mention legal ramifications.

Arjun dropped down to his knees, exhausted with the stress ripping his brain apart.

'Go apologize. Mend things with her. Beg for her forgiveness. Maybe she'll give in,' said the voice again.

'Never! That woman is out to destroy me and she'll stop at nothing. And I'll never bow down to her whims!'

The voice said nothing. Despite his inflated ego and disdain for women, Arjun knew there was no other way. Of course, he didn't care for redemption or forgiveness; he just wanted to claw himself out of this intricately woven web—the web called Maya.

As he quickly splashed his face with water, he remembered the day he had met Renu for the first time—a simple housewife who didn't have the voice to even speak up against her dominating father-in-law. Who would've thought she could transform into something as ferocious and deadly, threatening to bring down his entire existence?

'You always knew that about her, Arjun,' the voice reminded him.

Indeed, he had always known, ever since he had read her first book—her words, burning across pages. Her doe-like eyes were jaded, but their fire was hard to miss. He had seen it many a time. He had basked in its warmth when she took care of him. He had let it ignite his deepest passions when she had made love to him. It was there again, when she said she loved him and even tears couldn't extinguish it the day she fell to her knees, begging for him to stay. And he had decided to play with it. He couldn't have possibly gotten away with it unscathed.

He loosened the knot of his tie and picked the glass of water from the table to drink. Restless, he banged the glass on the table and sent the books crashing. Arjun was distinctly disturbed and his body language was proof of it. He got off the chair and started pacing around his office in acute frustration. He kept walking for what seemed like hours.

After a long time, Arjun went and sat in the plush leather chair in his office, and sat there contemplating the worst. This was his end. He had spent months playing games with Maya, but she, in one fell swoop had decimated him.

Checkmate.

TWENTY–SIX

Thunderous applause filled up the hallway as Maya walked through the entrance beside the stage. It was a moment hundreds of her readers had been waiting for. The place was so jam-packed that there was hardly any space to breathe. Crowds of people craned their necks to have a look at her or to click her picture. She looked resplendent in a translucent black saree and a bare-backed glittery blouse— just like everyone had imagined Maya to be. Her hair was styled in natural waves and even without too much make-up, her skin looked luminous. She walked in a confident gait to the sofas placed in the centre of the stage, but only she was aware of the nervous flutters in her chest. Leave alone addressing such a huge audience, she had never been on a stage before. But now was not the time to flinch. She was about to begin writing a new chapter of her life and give her destiny a direction she'd never thought she could.

Akriti squeezed her palm as she led her to the sofa, and Maya smiled at her. Even though Ravenhouse hadn't published Maya's book and for all technical reasons, Akriti wasn't supposed to be there, but there was no way she would have left her friend alone at such a critical juncture of her life. She knew that behind that diva-like facade was a shy, nervous woman who hadn't been out in the big bad world for a long time. And Renu wasn't prepared to leave her either, not after what she had done for her.

The frenzied applause from the audience did not die down even after Maya had seated herself on the sofa, with the session moderator on one side and Akriti on the other. She knew there would be difficult questions coming her way and she was prepared. There was nothing to hold her back now.

'This is an important moment in your career,' the moderator said cheerfully.

'Yes, even more so in my life,' Maya replied confidently. The crowd in front of her was now a noisy blur and all her attention was focused on the conversation. She was aware of the media covering the event and this was her big chance to establish her persona as Maya.

'We are all very happy to finally meet the woman behind our favourite bestsellers. What took you so long to come out?'

'Let's just say, my reality was holding me back. I was someone's wife, someone's daughter-in-law, a middle-class woman living in a close-knit society. Now I am none of those things. I am just a mother to two lovely children,' she said proudly.

'Don't your family members approve of your genre of books?'

'No, they don't.'

'What if you have to make a choice between writing what you do and playing the various roles a woman is supposed to play? What would you choose?'

'Like I said, I have already made my choice. I chose my craft. My role-play is done with, and I have only myself to be now.' Maya's voice grew more and more confident and triumphant as she spoke. Sitting beside her, Akriti was grinning with pride. She had known Maya would pull this off but never had she imagined that the timid, middle-class housewife she knew, was the same bold and confident woman that sat next to her on the stage!

Renu's heartbeats had settled to their regular pace and she sat back while answering the moderator. She had passed the test, done the unimaginable. Until that moment, she hadn't realized how far she had come. It sank in now, when she heard it from herself, not just in written words, but her voice too.

One year later . . .

It had been a while since Renu had spoken to Akriti; in fact, she had called her only once after reaching Ranikhet. 'Hey! How have you been?'

'You sound good! Much better than when I last heard your voice.' The happiness in Akriti's voice was evident. She knew that Renu had never lived alone, and now she had a life to run; all by herself. To gather the broken pieces of her soul and try to patch them back together. Akriti did not completely approve of Renu's choices but as a woman, she understood her pain. 'How's the writing coming along?' she asked.

'It's slowly coming back, Akriti,' Renu smiled. She knew that Akriti was genuinely concerned, because she believed in Renu's potential and nothing is more devastating for a lover of good stories than to see a pool of talent go to waste. Writing was Renu's only solace—the only thing she could call her own. Apart from her words and the pictures she painted through them, what else did she have?

'Tell you what? There's a friend of mine—also a writer. He just bought a retirement home in Ranikhet and moved there. Why don't you meet up with him sometime if you can.'

'Retirement home? How old is this friend of yours?' Renu jested.

'Does it matter?' Akriti laughed.

'No, it doesn't. I'll meet him if you insist. I could anyway do with a bit of like-minded company around here.'

Akriti messaged Renu the address and phone number of one Mihir Rana right after their call. Renu contemplated calling him right away. From whatever little Akriti had told her, Renu gathered that he was an old man, probably in his sixties, who had moved to the hills to escape the frantic pace of life in Delhi. He had been a professor of literature for several years, but now wanted to spend his time writing and doing social work in the area. Renu had not asked any more questions about him; neither had she asked why Akriti wanted her to meet him. He lived alone and was new to the place, could do with some company, just like her. Renu trusted Akriti enough to believe that this Mihir Rana must be a nice man if she was asking him to go see him.

Also, now that her identity was out in the open, Renu thought it was the right time to meet other people from the fraternity and build a good network, something she hadn't been able to do in Lucknow.

~

'Hi! You must be Maya?' Renu looked up from the table to find a stranger standing next to her. Mihir Rana was nothing like she had imagined at all.

'Renu . . .' she quickly corrected him and proffered a hand. He was probably in his late forties, not handsome in a conventional sort of way, but there was a certain charisma about his personality and the way he spoke.

'Akriti told me a lot about you,' she continued with a polite smile, hoping she had not come across as rude.

'Haha. I hope it was all good stuff. At least some of it,' he laughed with a friendly twinkle in his eyes. Renu couldn't help but notice the tinge of pain behind the twinkle.

Something about his aura made Renu feel instantly at ease. Given the past year of an almost isolated existence, it wasn't easy for her to talk to a stranger, leave alone open up to one. But Mihir seemed to be different. It didn't feel like she was meeting this man for the first time because their conversation started like old friends catching up after a long time and picking up right where they left off. She didn't know much about him or his past, but he just felt familiar.

'Yes, all good stuff,' Renu replied with a smile. 'I couldn't imagine anyone saying anything otherwise about you.'

Mihir looked a little embarrassed, as if not used to compliments. 'So what brings you here?' he asked, trying to change the subject.

'Well, long story short—a dead marriage, an affair gone bad, and a lucky run into some money to make up for it all,' Renu replied, surprised at what she had just said. This wasn't like her at all. Mihir laughed heartily at her response.

'Brevity is indeed the soul of wit, Maya!' he said, in between guffaws. 'Can I call you Maya, if you don't mind?'

'Ah, okay, you can.'

'And what about you?' she continued.

'Me? A bad marriage, an ugly divorce and savings lost to alimony,' he replied and they both laughed their hearts out again.

It had only been a few minutes since she had met Mihir but she could feel something churn within her. The world looked different—vibrant, happier and full of hope. She couldn't remember the last time the world looked like that to her. She didn't know where she was heading, but for some strange reason, she felt incredibly happy to meet Mihir.

The two began to meet often and the relationship grew. Neither of them knew what to call it, and after a while they stopped trying to give it a name because it was beautiful just the way it was.

In Mihir, she soon found a mentor and a guide. He was someone who would listen patiently, without judgement and without offering advice unless asked. In talking to him, she often found herself answering her own questions, while he smiled on knowingly. His presence had somehow grounded her being, and his words had the power to anchor the reckless boat that was her mind. With him, she felt calm.

~

Arjun stood at the edge of the cliff, looking down at the bottomless valley, which seemed to be calling out to him. The voices in his head echoed cruelly as every memory of Maya flashed before his eyes. Every wound, every betrayal and every lie flashed before his eyes. He wasn't one to be shaken by the call of the conscience for he had none, but Maya had left him with nothing to live for. She had taken away his reputation, his identity and all the respect he had gathered over the years. Every time her face flashed before his eyes, he tasted blood in his mouth. He had lived a colourful life, with harems of women tending to his every whim but as he stood there, counting his last moments, he realized how alone he was. There would be no one to miss him when he was gone. He would just fade into oblivion, like everybody else. Nobody would even shed a tear for him and he would be quickly forgotten.

His tormented mind was pushing him to just take that one step and end the agony once and for all. He would then be free.

Just then his phone vibrated in his pocket. It was an unknown number. Arjun rejected the call. He was in no mood to answer calls from unknown people, or anyone for that matter. He just wanted to spend the last moments of his life in peace before he took the final plunge.

The phone rang again, a different number this time. Arjun rejected it again, but the caller was persistent. Finally exasperated, Arjun decided to pick it up.

'Hello, am I speaking with Mr Arjun Singh Chauhan?' said a female voice.

'Yes. That's me . . . Who is this?' he asked curtly.

'Sir, I've been trying to call you to discuss the possible acquisition of your firm, Ravenhouse Publishers, by Gilmore Publishing.'

Arjun's ears suddenly perked up. Gilmore Publishing was the same firm that had released Maya's latest title. What would they possibly want from him? They were an established A-list publishing house. It just didn't make any sense.

'Acquisition? What do you mean? Don't you know that Ravenhouse is running into heavy losses? We are doomed. We are headed for devastation!' It was probably the first time in his life that Arjun was speaking the truth from his heart. On a regular day, he would have unleashed his Machiavellian magic to fleece whatever he could out of this loss-making deal but not today.

'We are aware, sir. But our stakeholders are adamant.'

'And why would they be? What could they possibly gain out of this?'

'I'm afraid I cannot discuss any details over the phone, sir. Would you like to schedule a meeting with our people?'

Arjun took a moment to reply. Maybe he still had a chance to get out of this mess and cut his losses.

Things moved at a pretty fast pace from there. Arjun met the business head and legal representatives from Gilmore Publishing and they offered him a deal that seemed like a pittance, but at that moment, it was the only way out. They were willing to buy out his entire publishing house, along with the wasteful stock of Kamini's book in the godown which by themselves were worth quite a bit. He was told that the owners lived abroad, and the power of attorney rested entirely with their lawyers in India. Arjun, however, couldn't be less bothered about any of those nitty gritties. He was getting a chance to retrieve something out of a loss-making situation and get the dead weight of this firm off his shoulders. That would be some slap on Maya's face. Who the hell did she think she was to go about plotting his destruction? He would show her now. And he also couldn't believe why anyone would be so foolish enough to hop aboard a sinking ship. But that, of course, wasn't his deal to worry about.

It didn't take too long for the paperwork to get signed and sorted, and soon enough, Arjun was no longer the owner of Ravenhouse Publishers.

It had been a long while since he had slept peacefully and he was glad that everything was behind him now.

Dawn broke and it was a start of a new day for him. He wasn't completely broke and he could start his life afresh, preferably in another city. He stumbled out of bed and made his way to the door to collect the newspaper. As he flipped through the pages over his morning cup of tea, he came across a headline that made his blood run cold.

'Bestselling author Maya buys out her former publisher!'

'What the hell is happening?' It was Kamini bellowing over the phone. Here she was, hoping to resurrect her non-existent career

as a writer by stealing Maya's manuscript but her best-laid plans had gone awry. She had invested so much in her relationship with Arjun just so that his publishing house would back her career but now, he was dismantled to bits and utterly useless to her cause.

'Well, at least we got our money,' he said, trying to pacify himself rather than her.

'Money? Do you even know what's going on? That bitch has initiated a merger between Gilmore and Ravenhouse. Do you understand what that means?'

It hit him like a bolt of lightning, rattling his insides. In that instant, he understood what Maya had been doing. She was showing him his place, wielding power over him and then destroying whatever was left of him with her benevolence. It was as if she had dangled him off a cliff and then pulled him back, as a mere display of strength. A cat chasing a mouse, pinning it down and then letting it go.

TWENTY-SEVEN

Renu opened the door and her heart sank to the pit of her stomach. 'Arjun!'

'Hi, Renu.'

'Why are you here? What do you want now?' Renu's eyes welled up with tears as her voice choked up. No matter how far she had come along, Arjun always made her weak from within.

'May I?' he asked.

'Come in,' she stuttered, unsure of how to feel about his abrupt reappearance. It had been more than a year since they parted ways and yet, her heart was pounding in his presence as rapidly as it always did.

Arjun found a place for himself on a couch in the drawing area. The cottage was plush and spacious, with floors of wood and tastefully done up interiors. The professional touch of an interior designer was quite apparent, and yet the home had a style that was reminiscent of Renu's own persona. There was a certain warmth and beauty in that house that only a woman in love with her space could lend, and which was clearly absent in her previous house. Those heaps of books, which had once been crammed into a dusty bed-box, now held an honourable place in a wall-to-wall bookshelf, along with new ones to give them company. There was bold colour on the walls, kitschy decor pieces, a huge painting of a woman's silhouette contorted into a sensual pose and mismatched furniture that seemed to perfectly fit together, just like different facets of the woman who had brought them together. A French window overlooked the valley, with a small village nestled further down.

However, the glamour of the house couldn't let Arjun tear away his eyes from Renu. She looked resplendent in a bright, well-fitted kurta and a pair of jeans, and, her face had a glow that he had never seen before. Her face was sullen and tense but her eyes had that sparkle that had mesmerized him the first time they met. But that's not how he remembered them after his last meeting with her. When he tore her apart with his words and watched those beautiful eyes go dead and sink into their sockets right before him.

He got up from the couch and held her hand, as if instinctively drawn to her.

Renu looked at him almost indifferently.

She knew it would end. She had always known it would never last. For how can anything that never even existed for real in the first place? It was all make-believe.

Quite heartbreakingly, she also knew that Arjun would live within her forever. It wasn't the first time that she was losing her rationality to instincts, but until now, the latter had never felt so primal. So animalistic. In that moment, she wasn't feeling love, or even lust for Arjun. It was a strange emotion—an impulsive urge to make love to him so intense that her raw feminine scent would haunt his senses forever. To unleash her womanhood on him with such ferocity that no other woman, no matter how hard she tried, would ever be able to overwrite her invisible marks on him. He would never forget the searing heat of her fingers on his skin and her moans would echo in his ears for a long, long time to come. In her wild, dancing eyes, he would see the extent of insanity that love can drive you to. He could never love her, at least not in the way she wanted him to, but she would make sure he would never forget her.

Renu stretched out her hand to lock his fingers in hers and assertively pulled him closer until she could feel the warmth of his breath on her neck. His muscles were taut in anticipation and his right hand crept along the circumference of her waist while the other made its way down to the bottom of her hip, hitching her up so that their lips could meet. Hungry. Desperate. Starved. Passionate. She grabbed him by the hair and bore her eyes into his, like they always did when they kissed. Except this time, her passion didn't feel pure. It was tinged dark with sorrow, resentment, pain, grief and an impending loss. In this moment, she was that proverbial flame burning at its brightest before going out for good.

He pinned her against the wall, kissing her mouth feverishly and his hands slipped under her kurta and glided across her waist to the arch on her lower back. She gasped; part in surprise and part in rapture. He knew his way around her body and the dampness between her legs was evidence of that. She unbuttoned her jeans and stepped out of them quickly as he pinned her against the wall once more. He pushed the fabric of her panties aside and his fingers made their way into her warm, slippery wetness. Renu moaned and pushed her hips forward, taking in as much of him into her as she could. His fingers danced playfully inside her, gently at first and then more intensely. He teased her nub mercilessly, her body convulsing in waves, with his arm supporting it at the small of her waist. He unbuttoned his jeans and entered her without wasting any time. She had missed the way his hands gripped her hair as he moved inside her, the friction of his damp skin against her own.

When he was done with her, she felt hot tears stream down her cheeks. They were tears of heartbreak and of catharsis.

'I have found her, Maya. I have found the woman I love.'

Her insides clenched in agony but she kept up a calm face; almost cold and indifferent.

'That's good to know. Treat her well. Don't treat her like you've treated me.' She didn't really mean to say the last sentence aloud but what was left to lose? She never had Arjun anyway, and now he had found his solace in the arms of another woman.

'How have I treated you?' Arjun's tone was suddenly defiant and indignant, which was so typical of him.

'The way you treat all women, with contempt and utter disdain. You have no respect for women, Arjun, and you are incapable of giving or receiving love.'

'Don't say that, Renu. You are the woman I love. You are mine. You know it, you have always known it. You proved me wrong. You broke my myth. I am capable of love too. You showed me!'

Renu stood still as if struck by a bolt of lightning. Her eyes looked blank but her mind was on an overdrive, playing and replaying every word Arjun had ever said to her and every action of his that didn't match up to those words. She relived every confusion, every question, and every delusion that had tormented her mind, all because of him. His lies rang in her ears, each hurtful word fresh as ever and today, as he stood before her with his handsome face and magnetic charm, he stank of betrayal. She still loved him, there was little doubt about that, but she could not bring herself to respect and trust him any more. She couldn't forget how he had derided and demeaned her, controlled and crushed her, twisted her will and tamed her fire, chained down her spirit and choked it so she couldn't breathe. Renu smirked a little at how quickly that thought untangled all her other thoughts, and wasn't that a refreshing change?

She also relived the peace and freedom that being alone had brought her over the past months. The surge of creative inspiration, the freedom of living and breathing in a space where she belonged. A life she could call her own. Dev might have left her alone, but Arjun had shown her what loneliness felt like at its worst.

For the very first time, his intense eyes failed to melt her heart. She took a deep breath and steadied herself.

'I might be yours, Arjun, but you are definitely not mine. Not any more anyway.'

'I am! You know I need you. And I know you need me.'

Renu burst out in loud laughter. 'Need! Arjun, I don't want a man who needs me. Enough people need me. Someone needs me to run their house, someone needs me to pay the school fees, someone needs me to put food on the table, and others need me to write good books. I don't need any more needy people. I want someone who WANTS me, who desires me and who loves me the way I deserve to be loved. The way I am capable of loving them back. I don't need crumbs of affection any more, I want the whole pie, Arjun and you can't give it to me because you are simply not enough to satiate my hunger, at least not for long. Not any more.'

Arjun's face hardened. 'What has happened to you, Renu? Am I not who you always wanted? How can you . . .?'

'Yes, you were what I wanted once upon a time. Were! But I think I was never in love with you, Arjun. I was in love with the idea of you and I am glad it was you because no one other than you could have shattered that illusion so violently. Maybe I would've survived on the few good memories alone but you snatched that away too by coming here today.'

'You will regret this, Renu. Don't come to me later begging me to take you back because I will not.'

'Don't worry. That ship has long since sailed and sunk. I can only wish well for you.'

Arjun let out a grunt and turned towards the door.

'Wait, Arjun, I have something for you.'

'What, now?'

Renu disappeared into a room and walked out with something in her hand. 'Here,' she handed him a book. *Maya*.

While Arjun fixed his glare on the cover of the paperback, Renu fixed hers on him. It gave her a secret kind of dark pleasure as Arjun's face contorted in anger and defeat as he read his rival publisher's name on the side, but couldn't utter a word.

Renu smiled and looked at her reflection in Arjun's eyes. All her masks had fallen off, all facades finally broken. She was no longer someone cowering under a false identity and neither was she someone who could be chained down and arm-twisted into submission. She was exactly who she was meant to be—a glorious bird in the sky with fire in her soul and ferocity in her heart; a soul free and fluid like the wind; wings wooing impossible dreams. She was no longer a bird in love with her cage. She was a phoenix resurrected. She was Maya.

'Before you leave, I want to thank you for what you have given me, Arjun.'

'What could that be? I have only given you pain.' Defeat outweighed remorse in Arjun's voice.

'You have given me, myself. I won't lie to you. I resent you as much as I love you. And I hate you for where you've brought me. But I'm also grateful for what you made me feel all this while. My love for you is stronger than anything else. I may push you off the cliff but I'll still break your fall because I may have the strength but I do not have the heart to destroy you. Some things are difficult to express because you don't have access to those emotions. But that doesn't mean that those emotions do not exist. You churned me inside out and took me to places within me that I did not even know existed. You made me feel, you made me yearn, you overwhelmed me, you gave me a million deaths and made me come alive. Now do you know why I had so much difficulty letting you go?'

'Oh, please keep your nonsense to yourself. I made you who you are today, Maya. Without me, you'd be nothing. NOTHING!' It was almost as if Arjun wasn't even listening to a single word she had said. He was enmeshed in his own thoughts. He'd never imagined that of all people, Renu would turn him down. Never had he felt so insulted. Just a few minutes ago, she'd made love to him like he was the only thing she ever wanted in the world, and then, she tossed him off like a used paper napkin. If that wasn't bad enough, she'd had the gall to flaunt her book in front of him; the book that could have saved Ravenhouse, the book she'd given to his rival publisher.

'I am what I am because I am good at what I do, Arjun,' Maya replied coldly, absolutely unaffected by Arjun's flaming eyes. 'In fact, if we talk of profits alone, I think you have benefitted from me way more than I have benefitted from you.'

This surely wasn't the Renu Arjun knew, the simple, sacrificing housewife who'd do anything for the sake of his happiness. He didn't know this shrewd, calculative woman who stood before him right now. It angered him that she missed no chance to show him his place now. After all, what wrong had he done that she was punishing him so?

'You think you're really smart, don't you,' he hissed. He wasn't about to leave without showing her HER place. Just who did she think she was?

'You think you've destroyed me? Haha. The truth is that it is I who have destroyed you!' he bellowed. It was very typical of Arjun to lose it the moment his ego was threatened. 'If it wasn't for Kamini and me, your marriage would've still been intact and you would be with your family, not rotting here alone!' he laughed.

Renu just looked at him plainly, for she already knew everything she had to. The two had set out to break her home, or rather break her. So she would spill herself out in the open. Kamini seduced Dev, while Arjun wove his web around her. They conspired against her just so that she would reveal herself to the public and make more money for their publishing house. If this had hit her some time ago, it would have probably sent her reeling in shock and yet another betrayal. But she had come too far now. Very far. She had pulled herself through her worst battles, scarred but unbroken. Nothing shocked or surprised her any more. She let out a little laugh as she pieced everything in her

mind to create a sordid picture where everyone had a knife
up her back.

'You didn't destroy me, Arjun, you liberated me. Look
at where you've brought me,' she gestured her hands
around the room they were standing in. 'I don't care how
I got here but every day I am thankful to god that I finally
did. Do you think I am rotting her alone? I have never been
happier and more at peace in my entire life, Arjun,' she said,
looking him straight in the eye.

Arjun looked down, a little embarrassed. He had seen
this woman at her weakest and now at her strongest, and
he had finally understood that there was nothing more he
could do to cause her any damage. He was defeated and
it pained Renu to see him that way, but then again, she
couldn't allow her weaknesses to surface. Not again. It had
taken a lot from her to come this far, and she had lost a
lot along the way; she wasn't going to live through all that
again, come what may, she promised herself.

'You gave me so much, and I could give you only pain,'
he said finally, with a tinge of remorse in his eyes.

'It's all right, Arjun. I let it go. You should let it go
too,' she said and wrapped her arms around him in a hug, to
which he reluctantly reciprocated. 'You should leave now,'
she whispered.

Renu waited till he was out of sight before she let
herself go. She couldn't stop the streams of tears that were
burning her eyes and neither could she suppress the grief
that was eating her up from within. The grief of losing what
she never had.

TWENTY–EIGHT

The skies above the Kumaon ranges were as blue as could be. Even the clouds here seemed to have a spirit of their own. They would dance around forming spellbinding patterns, sometimes like neatly arranged rows of cotton balls, and at other times stretching wildly across the horizon in careless abandon. Every evening, as the sun set behind the Nanda Devi peak, painting the sky tangerine, a part of Renu would heal.

Moving to Ranikhet was perhaps the best decision she had taken for herself. It was probably the only thing she had done solely for herself.

Her instincts had brought her to this place and it was for a good reason. The cosy two-bedroom cottage she had rented was poetically placed on a gentle hill slope overlooking the magnificent Himalayas, with the Nanda Devi peak gloriously towering in the distance. She was away from her family, society, Arjun and everything that had chained her down. Here, she was alone with her thoughts and her words. Words that had abandoned her for months. The fresh unpolluted fragrance of pines cleansed the poison from her skin, bit by bit, and with every gush of mountain breeze, she could feel her dormant creativity stirring back to life.

'You are made for great things, Maya. You just have to rein in your mind,' Mihir's words echoed softly in her thoughts and a fond smile spread across her lips.

Here in the hills, mornings were not harried. There was no one waiting impatiently for tea, no children to be packed off to school. Renu would still wake up early as usual but instead of tying her hair in a messy bun and breathlessly going about her morning rituals, she would dress up, lay out a yoga mat on the small lawn, close her eyes and breathe in the purifying scent of pines and mountains as the sun peeped out from behind the mountains and seeped into her being with its warmth.

She had initially felt guilty about sending Aneisha and Avi to a hostel but they were just a few miles away from her. She could go and meet them anytime she wanted and they spent most of their weekends at home with her, unless there were exams to study for. Aneisha was doing much better here than she was at her old school.

'Thank you, Maa, for getting me out of there,' she had told Renu after a few weeks of joining her new school. Continuing at her old school had become stressful for Aneisha, especially after Renu's meeting with her teachers.

She would always feel anxious about her teachers and peers judging her, and despite all her attempts to focus on academics, her grades were showing little signs of improvement. Once a lively, chirpy girl, she had withdrawn from all her friends and was quieter around the house too. Avi seemed to be quite unfazed by the changes happening around him, and Renu sometimes wondered if it was his extraordinary coping skills or if reality hadn't really sunk into his innocent, carefree heart. Nevertheless, he seemed to be loving his new environment.

Within weeks, seeds of stories were germinating from the dark corners of her mind. Her thoughts were beginning to toe her line. The chaos inside her had finally found some kind of order.

Love makes itself obvious. As does the lack of it.

Solitude brings isolation and sometimes that's all you need to gather your pieces and put them back together. Of course, they never fitted in the same order but they still made for a mismatched mosaic, which was magical in its own way.

She wasn't out to heal herself. She perhaps didn't want to. She wanted her wounds to bleed until they poured out of her fingers as her words. Because what else is prose, but pain packaged beautifully? But every time she sat down to write, words failed her, and the blackness followed her through days and nights. It frustrated her because it was all there, swimming like disjointed fragments in her head and yet it refused to spill out on paper.

'It's just not coming to me, Mihir. I'm scared I'll never be able to write anything coherent any more!' she said, exasperated as they sat in the corner of the small coffee shop. That's where they always sat, right from the first time they met. By now even the waiters knew their respective orders by heart. A lemonade for Maya and a beer for Mihir. They didn't serve beer in the cafe but Mihir paid them extra to get it from the liquor store down the street and allow him to have it there. He was eccentric like that.

'Maybe because there's too much of you in it?'

'What do you mean?'

'It's difficult to write a story when you are right in the middle of it. It becomes easier when you walk away from it and view it from a distance.'

Maya knew what he was talking about but she wasn't too happy with his answer. She just had to write. That's it. That was all she had and she was nothing without it.

Mihir was the only one she had shown her manuscript to because she knew he was probably the only one who could understand her language and read between the lines, and grasp the nuance of every word.

'I've read the draft, Maya. It is as chaotic as a broken heart.'

'It is not the chaos of a broken heart, Mihir. It is the fatigue of my soul. An inexplicable weariness that comes from chasing something elusive. Something that probably doesn't exist.'

'What are you chasing, Maya?'

Maya looked at him from across the coffee table, her mind grappling for a convincing answer. What was she chasing? What did she want? There were so many questions she had yet to ask herself. Did she want Arjun? The answer was in the negative. Despite what she felt for him, she didn't want him. Arjun could never fulfil her. He would always be a thorn stuck in her heart, but never in her reality. What did she want then? Did she want love? Yes, maybe she did. She wanted love. She wanted to be loved, for who she was and not for what she did for others. She wanted to be loved, the kind of love poets wrote symphonies about. She wanted the all-consuming, all-encompassing love that renders every single banality of mundane human existence irrelevant. The kind that explodes like a supernova and dispels all darkness. The kind that strips you down to your bones and makes you face your bare naked self, but with the warm comfort of a blanket that engulfs you when you begin to feel too vulnerable. The kind that merges two souls in such a way that it is difficult to tell one apart from the other. But does such a love exist for real? It probably doesn't. Was she chasing yet another illusion?

'You know something, Maya?' Mihir interrupted her thoughts. She focused her gaze back on him realizing it had been a while since she'd been drifting away with her thoughts. 'Between happiness and sadness, there's a middle road called peace. That's probably the one you need to take.'

Maya smiled faintly as she took a moment to let those words penetrate her. 'Here's to peace,' she said and raised her glass of lemonade. Mihir obliged by clinking his beer mug against her glass, and they both broke into jaded laughter.

'Writers are a blessed lot, Maya. Do you know why?'

'Tell me,' Maya replied with a faint smile on her lips

'Because, we hold the power to turn every grief, every loss and every wound on our soul into hard cash.'

This time around, their laughter wasn't jaded. It was uproarious. Maya realized she hadn't laughed like that in years. Her sides were aching and there were tears in her eyes.

'That's our glory and also our doom,' he added, his face suddenly growing sullen.

'Why doom now?' Maya looked at him quizzically, like she always did when he came up with his own answers to deep existential questions. He would say the craziest things, and yet they would make profound sense. She would soak in every word he said, every thought of his, only to replay it again and again in her mind till she could grasp the complete essence of it.

'Yes, doom. Because, we lose ourselves twice. First time when we live through it and then again when we write about it. So whatever kills us, kills us twice.'

It amazed Maya how he could talk about everything so easily without batting an eyelid, like he was giving a sermon at some writing workshop. He was always brimming with speech and yet there was so much left unexplored and unabsorbed. Maya often found herself running short of senses to soak him in with when he was in one of those moods.

Later in the evening, as Maya sat out in her balcony watching the crimson skies slowly turn dark, Mihir's words echoed within her and then it came to her. In a single blinding epiphany, she understood what had been holding her back. She was stuck because she was trying to sugar-coat reality, trying to turn thorns into petals out of her own sheer kindness. Writing does not work like that. If you do it right, it can be a brutally painful process that rips apart your insides and forces you to face your demons, look them in the eye and then find the courage to dance with them. She would have to be true to herself and write with full honesty, even if it meant dying all over again. She would have to bleed out words until her veins ran dry. She would have to script her story the way it was, and not the way she wanted it to be or the way she saw it. Not all stories have a beginning and an end, because they are not stories at all. They are journeys.

TWENTY–NINE

It had been many years since Renu had left home and moved to the mountains. They were lonely years, but none the lonelier than the rest of her life had been. They were also the most prolific, and perhaps also the most peaceful. She wrote eight books in this time—all bestsellers. Her name was everywhere and her identity was no secret. She graced covers of international magazines and made more money than she could have ever imagined. Her days were spent lost between her words, and her nights haunted by an absence of something unknown. She would fall into the deep dark abyss of her soul and emerge every morning, with an incoherent bunch of words to be woven into stories. It drained her but she would keep at it every day, battling the fatigue and trying to fill up the emptiness inside her with words.

It was just another evening in her life and there she was in the balcony, enviously watching the sun paint the sky red before it disappeared for the day only to light her up again in the morning. She called up Aneisha. Talking to her daughter always seemed to put her at rest, even if only for the moment. She was proud that her daughter had grown into a strong, independent woman. She ran an NGO that helped abandoned women. Maya had always known that her daughter was made for big things. She had that fire in her, and the kindest heart. And Avi was training to be a pilot like he always wanted to be. It was only a matter of time before he would claim the skies. After spending an hour on the phone with Aneisha, she called up Avi too. He was out partying with his friends but he stepped out of the pub to talk to his mother. Not only did both her children look after her, they looked out for each other too. Maya knew they would never be alone. She thought of calling Mihir but then dismissed the idea.

She drew the curtains of her room open before settling into bed. It was still early. The sun was still kissing the mountaintops, painting myriad pictures, a different one each day. Like every day, she would read herself to sleep. It would take a while because unlike words, sleep didn't come easy to her. Pills were her loyal companion and she reckoned she would need one today. She could feel something sinking within her. It was a familiar feeling—one that visited her every night. The weight sitting on her chest, making it impossible for her to breathe. She gasped for air but it only got worse. There was no way to silence those noises in her head suddenly, like a bunch of rowdy hooligans pulling her in different directions, tearing her limbs apart, assaulting her. They all reminded her of her lonely, loveless existence. She travelled back in time to her lonely childhood, the moments she spent talking to herself because there was no one else, the dreams she'd woven with Dev and the slow painful death they suffered. She thought of Arjun—the love she'd always longed for, and the love that turned to dust the moment she thought she had it in the palms of her hands with him. Abandonment, indifference, betrayal, worthlessness—all came to haunt her in a single moment like a pack of demons until she could no longer bear the weight of her own existence.

She needed to sleep. Sleep was the only escape. She popped a pill out of the pack, a bright blue one. Then two. Then three. Until the whole pack was done. She quickly washed them down with a single gulp of water from the bottle sitting on her bedside table. There were other things sitting there too. A stack of books she loved to read at bedtime. The ones that understood her and the ones she understood. Hemingway, Plath, Virginia Woolf, Anne Sexton. There was also one of her own. The one with a black cover and red font that said *Maya*. Her best work. Her eyelids began to grow heavy and her gaze grew vacant as she stared outside the window, as if waiting for someone or something that would never come. The sun had set.

~

'How are you feeling, Maya?' a gentle voice spoke as Renu opened her eyes. Her eyelids felt heavy, her vision felt blurred and her head felt like it would shatter into pieces if she tried to lift it off the pillow. She still struggled to make sense of her surroundings. Despite the objects in the room swimming across her field of vision and the mid-day sunlight piercing her eyes, she could clearly recollect what had happened the night before.

'How long have I been gone?' she whispered, deliberately not looking the doctor in the eye.

'A little over a day but don't worry, you are all right now,' the doctor said.

She knew she had drifted too far, but something had pulled her back in those last moments before she lost consciousness. The thought of her children, and perhaps Mihir, had made her bolt out of the bed and into the bathroom to throw up the medication she had ingested in a moment of impulse. Exhausted and sick, she had just about managed to call Dr Shah, her trusted doctor, before slumping back into bed and passing out.

Her insides felt queasy, as if they would revolt against her any moment.

'Can you please call Mihir and ask him to come over?' she requested, handing Dr Shah her phone, unable to talk much.

'He's already here. He came today morning asking after you, but I sent him out to get some medicines,' Dr Shah said with a gentle smile. 'I think I can leave now. You give me a call if you need me.'

Renu nodded, before drifting back to sleep again.

When she woke up, she found Mihir sitting beside her, caressing her arm gently, letting her take the time she needed to regain her composure. Even though she had wanted him by her side, a cacophony of thoughts erupted in her mind seeing him there.

You just need to rest,' he replied with a reassuring smile, quite matter-of-factly, as if nothing too grave had happened. His calmness left her a bit flummoxed. He obviously knew why she'd been unconscious for that long. What would he be thinking of her? And how would she explain herself to him if she had to? In that moment, more than her pounding head and lurching stomach, she was worried about how Mihir must be judging her and once again, her mind filled up with guilt and pitiful self-loathing.

'I . . . you . . .' she fumbled for words but couldn't find any that could save the situation.

'Shhh. Don't say anything. Let's get you back on your feet first. There will be a lot of time later to do any talking you want to do,' Mihir said softly and bent forward to plant a kiss on her forehead. Renu closed her eyes.

There was always something calming about his presence and in an instant, all her apprehensions vanished. He got up from the revolving chair he had pulled into her room from her study and walked out of the room. Once again, her heart filled with dread. *Was he leaving, now that she was conscious again? After all, who in his right mind would want to associate with someone like her? Someone who was weak and irresponsible and . . .*

The voices in her head died down when he walked back into the room with a plate in his hands. 'I am not much of a cook but I've tried to whip up something. You need to eat something now that you are awake.'

Renu smiled weakly at him. She struggled to prop herself up on the bed because her limbs felt heavy. Mihir put the plate on the side table and proceeded to help her up, placing a few pillows behind her for support. He then pulled out a foldable breakfast table from beside the bed. She peered into the plate—it had *daal chaawal* but the way Mihir had plated it, it looked no less than a gourmet meal at a five-star restaurant. It had a garnish of freshly chopped coriander and a side of salad, which was essentially an eclectic mix of ingredients carved out in the shape of animals. The sight of it made Renu smile. 'I used to make wood sculptures some time ago. Thought it wouldn't hurt to try it out on carrots and cucumbers for a change. Turned out pretty neat, eh?' he asked. He watched her as she struggled to pick up the spoon. Her movements were uncoordinated and her body seemed limp, like she was having trouble even sitting straight. Mihir took the spoon from her hand and she slumped back into the pillows, closing her eyes briefly. He gave her a minute to relax before bringing a spoonful of food close to her mouth.

'I'll eat myself, Mihir. You really don't have to . . .' she resisted groggily, feeling a little embarrassed at being treated like a baby.

'Shush, woman . . .' Without saying another word he placed his finger on her lips. His eyes said everything; he wasn't about to take no for an answer.

She reluctantly took a spoonful of food into her mouth but she couldn't taste a thing. She swallowed it anyway because she didn't want Mihir's efforts to go to waste. Her stomach churned a bit with the first bite but it settled down after a couple more. She realized she hadn't eaten anything in almost two days, and the warm home-cooked food made her feel slightly better.

'Feeling better, love?' Mihir asked tucking a stray lock of hair behind her ear. The food definitely made her feel better and she nodded with a slight smile. She still felt weak but a lot calmer and settled within.

'You should sleep it off now. I'm sure you'll be okay by tomorrow. If you feel better in the evening, we can go for a short walk, or just sit outside for a while. Would you like that?'

'Yes, I'd love to. It seems like ages since I watched the sunset,' she said.

'I'll see you in the evening. You rest in the meanwhile and remember, I am just a call away, okay?' Mihir smiled at her before he turned to leave the room, but Maya held his hand.

'Do you have some work to do?' she asked.

'No. I don't. Nothing too important anyway,' he replied.

'Can you stay with me here a little longer?' It wasn't like Maya to ask anyone for anything, not any more. Her mind went back to Arjun. And Dev. And how she had begged and pleaded for their love and attention. She would never let herself be rejected like that again, she had promised herself. She would never ask for or accept anything that wasn't freely given to her. And yet, in that moment, she felt vulnerable and she realized that somewhere without knowing or making a conscious effort, she had begun to trust Mihir.

'Yes I will, but only if you promise to try and sleep for some time. Your body needs healing.'

'Lie down next to me?' Maya placed a hand on the bed beside her, her voice quivering with trepidation, wondering what he would think.

Mihir, however, seemed totally unperturbed by her request, like she had asked him for the most natural thing in this world. He slipped into the sheets rights next to her, placing his arm under her head and lowering her so that her head rested on his shoulder. He then wrapped his other arm around her, turning her slightly towards him to gently rub her back, kissing her forehead intermittently. Maya clutched at his shirt and dug her face into his chest. His smell was raw and comforting at the same time, and within minutes she drifted off to sleep.

~

When she woke up a few hours later, she still found herself there, in Mihir's arms. He was asleep too, but he had been careful not to move much.

She noticed that his feet were dangling from the edge of the bed and he still had his shoes on, but he was sleeping like a log. He had probably been awake all night looking after her.

Maya quietly slipped out of bed, took off his shoes and pulled the covers over Mihir. He flinched a little but settled back into deep sleep when Maya placed the palm of her hand over his forehead.

She had known Mihir for so long but she had never seen him asleep. He looked so different when he was asleep. When he was awake, it was hard to look past the depth in his intense eyes and his words even when he was talking about something mundane. When he talked, Maya listened with rapture. And when Maya talked, he understood. Everything she put into words and didn't. With him, she realized she could be her true self; she already was. In his presence, she felt happy and safe.

In the pinkish glow of the evening sun setting behind the hills, she took a few moments to absorb the man who had been her friend, confidant and guide and a lot more through these years. Even with his salt and pepper stubble, his face looked childlike as he slept. Looking at him, Maya realized how lucky she was to have him in her life and that had the pills done their job the other night, it would have been entirely her loss to part with someone who she treasured so much.

THIRTY

'You didn't question me even once,' Maya said as she and Mihir sat outside having tea in her little garden overlooking the mountain ranges. A few days had passed since the episode and Maya had slowly regained her strength. Mihir just looked at her and smiled. This had been their routine since years. Every evening, they would go for a walk together and on their way back, Mihir would stop over at Maya's place for tea or they would both go and sit at their usual place in the cafe.

It had all started very casually, on one of their walks in the woods. Maya had invited him in for a cup of evening tea out of courtesy and before they knew it, it had become a part of their routine. Even though Maya wasn't accompanying him on walks these days, she would still wait for him outside in her lawn with tea ready in a thermos. It was the time of the day she most looked forward to. There was a wrought iron garden swing there that Mihir really loved to sit on, so she made it a point that she sat on the cane garden chair so that Mihir could have his time on the swing. She found it amusing that he actually rocked it back and forth despite the creaking noises it made. 'Swings are meant to be swung, aren't they?' was his standard retort whenever he caught Maya staring and smirking at him. And then he swung even faster, with a silly boyish grin plastered on his face.

In that hour over tea, they would talk about every possible thing under the sun, from the mundane to the ridiculous.

Even though she had posed the question, in her heart she knew she was only seeking his validation. She already knew the answer.

'I didn't have to, Maya. I just wish I was here. Then all this wouldn't have happened,' he said. Maya knew he was right. She probably wouldn't have succumbed to that impulse if Mihir had been around. He was one man who knew his way around her darkness. He would have never let her sink.

'Please don't blame yourself. It was just one moment. I don't know what I was . . .'

Mihir placed his finger on her lips shushing her up. 'You don't have to explain anything.'

'Want to go inside?' she asked. He just had a T-shirt on him and even that was damp with sweat after the walk.

'I should be heading home, shouldn't I?' He got up reluctantly and stretched his arms over his head.

'Stay back for dinner?'

'What have you made today?'

'Soup. I'm on a diet,' Maya said cheekily.

'Perfect. I love soup!' Mihir replied, his crestfallen face belied the enthusiasm in his voice and it made Maya chuckle.

'There's some roasted chicken left over from yesterday. Will that do?' she said with a mischievous smile and he heaved a rather audible sigh of relief.

They settled into a couch in Maya's living room with a glass of wine and once again, conversation flowed and like always, they lost track of time. A couple of glasses later, Maya's eyelids began to weigh down. She wasn't very used to alcohol. She'd started drinking a bit only recently, and she only drank when she was with Mihir.

'You look sleepy. You should go to bed. It's late,' Mihir said softly, pushing a stray lock of hair away from her cheek and tucking it behind her ear. She shook her head in response.

'Want me to stay here with you till you are asleep?' Something about Maya's drunk eyes told Mihir that she wanted him around.

'Longer,' she whispered.

Mihir walked across to the table and picked up a bottle of water from the table. The ease with which he moved around her house reminded Maya of how long they knew each other and how close they were. Years of accumulated trust, shared joy, grief and friendship. Only the ache gnawing within her was new. She was looking at him holding the bottle of water high, neck turned upwards and stretched as he poured the water down his parched mouth. The muscles in his neck as the water rushed down his throat. Then for the first time, she let her eyes linger on his broad shoulders and back. His body held signs of an active youth, spent in playing rough and tumble field games. Mihir had paused now and was looking out of the window. Maya felt this enormous need to measure his back with her hands. And she wanted to wrap him up in her arms.

He turned around suddenly and looked at her. It made her avert her eyes briefly but they quickly returned to look at him. The stillness hung heavy between them. A breeze rustled up the curtains and send them swirling.

'Umm . . . I think I should leave,' Mihir said.

Maya mumbled incoherently. She was trying to tell him not to go but the words didn't leave her lips. Mihir picked up his coat from the sofa and walked to the door. His hand turned the doorknob, and then he stopped. He turned back and looked at Maya. It seemed like he was waging a war within himself. Maya's feet seemed to have a mind of their own. They walked towards Mihir, closing the space between them. They looked into each other's eyes, the storm so obvious. Maya moved first, her mouth searching for Mihir's. Then with a deep sigh they both kissed. It was warm, deep, sensual and slow. She savoured his wine-infused breath, his full lips. Her tongue slipped into his mouth and tangled wildly with his tongue. Her hands were holding his dear face, caressing his unshaven cheeks, their kiss deepening. They were nearer now and she could feel his length against her. His hand reached behind her to unclasp her hair. It barely came tumbling down her shoulders before he pressed his mouth into her neck, kissing her neck and shoulders.

A little later, the ensuing madness found them hungrily devouring each other. Maya stood with her hands on the living room wall. Mihir stood shirtless, tall and burly. He was kissing the back of her neck, his hands gripping her hips.

She drew herself closer to Mihir on the couch and clutched him by the back of his neck, burying her nose into his neck. Apart from the faint hint of cologne, he smelt raw, and his stubble grazed against her cheek. The soft symphony that her warm breath played on his damp skin compelled his hands to slide along the sides of her waist, pulling her closer and riding up to hold her by the back of her neck. They had been in close physical proximity so many times before but something about this moment felt explosive, like years of underlying sexual tension, which they had so cautiously kept to themselves, breaking all barriers and rising to the surface. There were still no words between them, no asking, no telling. She tugged at him and he instinctively knew what he had to do. It was something he'd wanted to do for the longest time but his fear of losing Maya had kept him away. He wrapped his fingers around her long raven hair and pulled it back gently, exposing her neck and her jawline. His lips were all too eager to taste her supple skin and soak in her feminine aroma. They plunged right in, igniting a dormant fire in her gut. Their breaths mingled and their lips locked, tasting each other gently at first and then sucking more impatiently, urgently. There was restlessness, but no rush. Each wanted to take time to savour the other, and indulge each sense, letting the flowing passion penetrate every pore of their being. It was Maya who led him to the edge of the room, but it was Mihir who pinned her to the wall. Maya let her arms drop in submission to his kisses, but Mihir lifted them up and held them above her head, locking her fingers with his. It was as if their bodies spoke the same language and their souls were perfectly in sync. Mihir's lips kissed the tender skin of her armpits before pulling the wide neckline of her tee to one side and grazing his lips against her bare shoulders before he went lower, kissing her breasts over her shirt and feeling them swell against his mouth. Maya arched her back and Mihir's hands swirled behind her, leaving her fingers to sink deep into his unruly salt and pepper hair and grab it almost violently. She took his lower lip between her teeth, playfully nibbling and thrusting, inviting his tongue to play with hers as his hands slipped under the hem of her shirt and glided across her bare skin. The hunger in his touch made Maya kiss him even deeper, grinding her body against his hitched up her shirt as he squeezed the curves of her waist. A soft moan escaped her as his fingers caressed her bare stomach, making circles around her navel.

'Take it off,' she gasped, and lifted her arms so Mihir could slide the shirt off her. She stood in front of him in a lacy black bra and denims while he sat on the couch, his palms grasping the sides of her waist, pulling her closer. A shudder ran down the length of her spine when he buried his face into her stomach, kissing it, nibbling it, with his tongue teasing her navel before plunging into its depth. It didn't take her much thought to slide his T-shirt off him, leaning against his body, their naked skins touching for the very first time in a delirious, electrifying moment. Grabbing him by the hair, she pushed his face deeper into her belly. She wanted to feel his naked skin against hers

His hands frantically unbuttoned her jeans, gliding around her waist and down the curve of her spine, cupping her ample bottom. The beltline lowered itself on its own, revealing her feminine contours. Mihir kissed her over her panties. They were damp and the raw musky scent sent his head into a tizzy.

He got up from the couch and swiftly lifted her up in his arms, carrying her to the bedroom. As he lowered her onto the bed, Maya sucked his lips into hers and dug her nails into the back of his shoulders. 'I want you,' she whispered breathlessly into his ears as her legs parted almost involuntarily. But Mihir was in no hurry. He was going to take his time with Maya, despite the heat between them running high.

Her hands went around him, caressing his back and broad shoulders. They continued to kiss, like they were running out of breath or the world was ending. Then she felt his large hand clasp her breast. Her breath caught in her chest. His touch hesitant at first, grew bolder. Mihir felt the weight of Maya's breasts in his palms. Arousal and tenderness for her coursed through him. He bent down and pressed his face into the softness of her breasts, breathing in the scent of her skin. Then a sudden urge took over and his mouth closed around her right breast, searching for her nipple through the thick fabric of her bra and sucked hungrily. Maya unhooked her bra and helped Mihir peel it away. The first instance of his hungry mouth on her breast made her moan loudly. Her hands curled into his salt and pepper hair as she looked down at him. The tenderness on her face was apparent as she watched Mihir's mouth suck on her nipple. Very soon, Maya was hurriedly unbuckling Mihir's pants. Eager to feel his hardness in her hands.

His fingertips sank into her calves, digging deep and moving upwards towards her thighs. She shuddered a little and moaned as his rough palms cupped her between the legs, his fingers getting drenched in her desire. He looked into her wide eyes and she nodded, parting her legs further, allowing him to slip in and explore her, as her head rolled back in delirium. She pulled him lower towards her, kissing him hungrily, sucking his tongue as he penetrated her depth with his fingers making her arch her back and place her hand over his, guiding him deeper.

She could feel his arousal press against her. When she couldn't wait any more, her hand wrapped itself around his hardness to guide him inside her.

Her moist tenderness told him that she was ready to take him in and despite his intense craving for her, Mihir wanted to be gentle. He held her by the back of her head as his manhood penetrated her depth. She whimpered as he glided in and out of her, sending her pelvic muscles into uncontrollable spasms. He was in no hurry and neither was she. They gazed deliriously into each other's eyes as they made slow, passionate love, savouring every moment and allowing their passion to simmer for a bit. Maya moved her hips perfectly in sync with Mihir's strokes, which grew faster and more urgent each second. She clutched at his shoulders and sucked on the palm of his hand to muffle the screams that were threatening to escape.

'Come for me . . .' he grunted.

'With you,' she whispered back.

He pounded faster when he felt her stomach clench in waves so intense that he could feel them coursing through his skin. He held her tighter when he felt her body shudder in pleasure and let go in that moment, filling her up. Breathless and panting, they lay spent in each other's arms till they drifted off into blissful slumber.

~

When Maya opened her eyes in the morning, Mihir was still there, half awake. She snuggled closer to him and soon their lips found their way to each other.

'Tea?' she asked, as if nothing extraordinary has happened the night before. She made her way to the kitchen and walked out with the tea, heading straight to the lawn because she was sure she would find Mihir there, on his favourite swing.

As she placed the tea on the table in front, Mihir shifted to one end of the swing and held out his hand. Maya placed her hand in his palm and he tugged at it softly to make her sit next to him on the swing. Almost instinctively, Maya rested her head on his shoulders. They sat like that for a while, close to each other, their fingers enmeshed without a word being exchanged between them. It felt calm and tranquil. In that blissful silence, time flew and the cool mountain breeze brought with it a slight chill that made the two of them huddle up closer. Mihir wrapped his arm around Maya, rubbing her shoulders. Although that did little to protect her from the cold, it was these little things he did that always warmed her from within. Gusts of cool mountain breeze teased their faces and Maya tried to remember the last time she had felt so much at peace. And so blessed. What she had been looking for, had been there all along.

Love should feel like clarity, not confusion
Comfort, not illusion
An ache, not pain
Longing, not loneliness
Love should feel whole

ACKNOWLEDGEMENTS

It was a chance conversation with a fellow author from Pakistan that sowed the seeds of this story in my mind. I was fascinated and curious as to why someone as talented and accomplished as she was would choose to write romances under a pen name. The answers were obvious—for most women in our society, it is anything but easy to express their desires, leave alone be accepted for them.

We as women unflinchingly give up so much of ourselves for the world around us, that somewhere down the road we forget who we really are and what we truly want. We all make sacrifices, for varied reasons and to varied degrees; but sacrifices we make, nevertheless.

Maya is not just one such woman. She is every woman. Every woman who had to give up her individuality for the sake of family and society. Every woman who had her dreams and desires stifled because the world around her would have none of it. Every woman who got much less than she deserved.

But here is what Maya is not—she is not a victim of her circumstances or a figure of pity, at least not for long. She is a woman of phenomenal inner strength and quiet rebellion. Much like a tea bag dipped in hot water, all it takes is a little push, before she comes into her own and unleashes her feminine power. And finds the courage to free herself— from the cage of desires.

For this, I thank every Maya I have ever known. In your strength and simplicity, you have been my inspiration.

Rishabh the Husband, for being the standard contributor of filmy twists to all my stories. And my life in general.

My family people, for being the wind beneath my wings. And also for not throwing a fit over the steamy sex scenes in the book.

Amit, my EP, for being there all along and beyond. You know and understand Maya like nobody else, and this book is as much yours as it is mine.

Kanishka, my agent. This book wouldn't have seen the light of the day without your support.

Vaishali, for showing faith in this story. And for helping me make it the best version of itself.

Paloma, for being such a sincere and meticulous editor.

Shwe. So much of Maya comes from you, and you know it.

Samarpita, who is rightfully the 'mausi' of this book. And also its very first editor.

For everyone who has been eagerly waiting for this— Maya is finally here!